BROTHER AGAINST BROTHER

BY PHYLLIS R. FENNER

Published by John Day Co. Inc.
OUR LIBRARY, The Story of a School Library That Works
THE PROOF OF THE PUDDING, What Children Read

Published by Alfred A. Knopf, Inc.
ADVENTURE, RARE AND MAGICAL
CRACK OF THE BAT
GIANTS AND WITCHES AND A DRAGON OR TWO
MAGIC HOOFS, Horse Stories from Many Lands
TIME TO LAUGH

Published by Franklin Watts, Inc.
GHOSTS, GHOSTS, GHOSTS
HEROES, HEROES, HEROES
HORSES, HORSES, HORSES
SPEED, SPEED, SPEED

ILLUSTRATED BY

William R. Lohse

Brother Against Brother

STORIES OF THE WAR
BETWEEN THE STATES

SELECTED BY

Phyllis R. Fenner

WILLIAM MORROW & COMPANY · NEW YORK

Grateful acknowledgment is made for permission to reprint the following:

"The Coverlid," by Mary Wells, from St. Nicholas Magazine. © 1922 by The Century Company. Reprinted by permission of Appleton-Century-Crofts, Inc.

"For the Honor of the Company," by Mary E. Mitchell, from The Atlantic Monthly. © 1911 by The Atlantic Monthly Company, and reprinted with their permission.

"The Home-Coming" and "The Battleground," by Elsie Singmaster, from her book, Gettysburg. © 1930, 1941 by Elsie S. Singmaster. Reprinted by permission of Houghton Mifflin Company.

"Silent Grow the Guns," by MacKinlay Kantor. © 1935 by The McCall Corporation. Reprinted by permission of MacKinlay Kantor.

"The White Feather," by Thomas Bailey Aldrich, from his book, Sea Turn. © 1902 by Thomas Bailey Aldrich; © 1930 by Talbot Aldrich. Reprinted by permission of Houghton Mifflin Company.

"The Banjo String," by Louis Reed, from The Atlantic Monthly. © 1933 by The Atlantic Monthly Company, and reprinted with their permission.

"Cadmus Henry, Balloon Observer," by Walter D. Edmonds, from his book, Cadmus Henry, published by Dodd, Mead and Company. © 1949 by Walter D. Edmonds. Reprinted by permission of Harold Ober Associates.

"Jack Ellyat at Gettysburg," by Stephen Vincent Benét, from his book, John Brown's Body, published by Rinehart & Company. © 1927, 1928 by Stephen Vincent Benét; © renewed 1955, 1956 by Rosemary Carr Benét. Reprinted by permission of Brandt & Brandt.

"The Day after Thanksgiving," by Harnett T. Kane, from his book, Spies for the Blue and the Gray. © 1954 by Harnett T. Kane. Reprinted by permission of Hanover House.

"Corporal Hardy," by Richard Ely Danielson, from The Atlantic Monthly. © 1938 by Richard Ely Danielson, and reprinted with his permission.

"Lincoln Speaks at Gettysburg," by Carl Sandburg, from his book, Storm Over the Land: A Profile of the Civil War. © 1939, 1942 by Harcourt, Brace and Company, Inc., and reprinted with their permission.

Fifth Printing, October 1963

ESF¬ 629
SC

With thanks to
Mary Karr Jackson,
for starting me
on my career with books.

THE WAR BETWEEN THE STATES

All wars are terrible but this was one of the worst. Families were divided. Brother fought against brother. It was sordid, without glory, and it left a bitter feeling in our country lasting to this day.

There are many stories about famous generals and statesmen of this period, but the real heroes were the people like you and me: the soldiers who suffered cold, hunger, wounds, imprisonment; the civilians who suffered heartache from divided loyalties and the loss of home and family. This is a collection of stories about them from both sides, and I hope they will give you a picture of what these everyday folks went through.

P. F.

Contents

BROTHER AGAINST BROTHER

The Coverlid

BY MARY WELLS

It lies along the back of the old mahogany davenport, the
coverlid, its rich blue and dull scarlet softened into only
greater beauty by passing years, for the coverlid dates
back to prerevolutionary times. The story has to do with
my own grandmother, Susan Howard Warren, and I tell
it as it has often been told to me.

Sue Howard was not yet fifteen in those summer days
when Lee's gray-clad troops swept up the eastern side of
the Blue Ridge, with Meade's men keeping dogged pace
at their right.

The Howard plantation was directly in the path of the
steadily advancing Union troops, and here, save for a few
Negro servants, Sue and Miss Cecilia, her father's oldest

sister, were alone, Colonel Robert Howard being with Pemberton in beleaguered Vicksburg and Lieutenant Tom Howard with Lee himself.

Sue's mother had died when Sue was a baby, leaving her little daughter to the care of gentle Miss Cecilia. Sue had grown up loving every spot of the old plantation and the surrounding country. One of her greatest pleasures was to ride with Tom or old Uncle Ephraim through the pine woods and up the winding mountain road to the cabin of Miss Alida Grant.

Through the small garden of carefully tended flowers, a path led up to the weather-beaten little dwelling. The quaint interior had a never-failing attraction for Sue. A wide fireplace lay along one side. On the floor were braided rugs. Over the mantel an old-fashioned clock ticked away the slow minutes. By the window overlooking the wide sweep of valley stood the armchair in which had sat Alida's father, grandfather, and his father before him. In one corner was the bed with its plump mattress of feathers; and there, spread so smoothly that not a wrinkle was visible, lay the coverlid.

What the shining old mahogany in the great Howard parlors, the yellowing lace of her grandmother's wedding veil, her grandfather's seal ring were to Sue, that and more was the coverlid to the gaunt old mountain woman, last of her race.

Sue and Alida often talked of the coverlid.

"It's wonderful, Miss Alida," said Sue, "but it must have been a lot of work."

Alida Grant nodded. "Grandma made it every bit herself back in Vermont when she was only sixteen. When my great-gran'ther found out that she and Thad Simmons were aiming to get married, he gave her half a dozen sheep as an engagement present. Thad sheared them, and the carding and spinning Grandmother did herself. Many a time I've heard her tell how soft and white the long rolls were. Next came the dyeing. Indigo and madder, she used. Some folks think cochineal gives a prettier red, but nothing could have kept its color better than this.

"After the Revolution, when Thad got his government grant, they came to Virginia. Grandma carried that mirror all the way, with the coverlid wrapped around it."

"It's a beautiful pattern, Miss Alida. Has it a name?" asked Sue, admiringly.

" 'Virginia Beauty,' most folks call it—chariot wheels and the double cross. There are a lot of fancier patterns, but, to my mind, this is the prettiest of them all. I've got the draft yet."

Alida went to the tall chest of drawers and took out a strip of yellowing paper which she carefully unrolled.

Sue bent over it curiously. "What funny little marks! They look just like the strokes Miss Rowley used to have us make in our copy books. I don't see how your grandmother could tell a thing about them."

"Each one of those little marks means something," said Miss Alida. "They're easy enough to figure out if you know anything about weaving. It's like picking out stitches in fancy embroidery. As for the coverlid, Grandma gave it to my mother when she was married, and, as I was the only girl, it naturally came to me. I set considerable store by it."

Miss Alida's gnarled hand rested caressingly on the beautiful folds.

After the outbreak of the war, Sue in her loneliness went more than ever to the little cabin on the mountainside. Not that she and Miss Alida had the same views. In all

Virginia, there was no stancher little Rebel than Sue, and, with the blood of New England forebears in her veins, Miss Alida was uncompromisingly Union. Strange as it may seem, their very differences drew them nearer together, and the young girl in her anxiety for father and brother found comfort in Miss Alida's homely counsel and rugged strength.

All through the early summer of 1863, there had been rumors of a Confederate advance, and at last rumor merged into certainty. One June morning, Negro Ben rushed excitedly into the great hall where Miss Cecilia and Sue were sitting.

"De Yanks are comin' dis time fo' shuah, Miss Cely. Mass Holland's Joe done see 'em ovah by de ford, big guns, baggage wagons, and all. Dey're aimin' to head off Gineral Lee."

Miss Cecilia and Sue hurried out on the porch. In the silence of the summer morning, listening, they could hear far away a dull, continuous rumble. Miss Cecilia's delicate face grew pale.

"I hope they'll go by the lower road," she said.

Even as she spoke, at the bend beyond the woods, there arose a cloud of dust, and, galloping up the road, came a troop of blue-coated cavalry. With a jingle of spurs and a clank of sabers, they swept up the driveway to the porch. The leader, a young soldier with the bars of a first lieutenant, swung himself from his horse. At the foot of the steps he paused and took off his cap, bowing low. Sue noticed the glint of the sun on reddish-brown curls and the lines of weariness in the young face.

"Madam," he said, addressing Miss Cecilia, who stood slenderly erect, "the day is hot; my men are tired and thirsty. If you will kindly tell us where we can find water?"

Miss Cecilia turned to the gray-haired old Negro at her back. "Ephraim," she said, with calm dignity, "show this— gentleman the well. Sue, come into the house."

"Dis way, sah," said the old Negro, respectfully; and following his guidance, the company rode around to the rear of the mansion.

The young lieutenant lingered, his eye on Sue.

"I have a little sister just about your age up in York State," he said, a little wistfully.

Sue thought of Tom, also riding north through the summer day. In her imagination, somehow, she had never pictured Yankees as pleasant-faced young men with little sisters. Despite herself, her heart softened toward the enemy.

"Her name is Mary," went on the young man. "I have her picture here." From his breast pocket he took a little velvet case and handed it to Sue.

Instinctively she took the daguerreotype. A merry-faced little girl with a wealth of curly hair looked up at her.

"Her hair's red, too," said the soldier, with a smile; "runs in the family."

"Sue, my dear," came Aunt Cecilia's voice in surprised accents.

"Yes, Aunty," answered Sue; then, "Wait a minute!" she commanded the young man. She ran into the house, and shortly returned with a pitcher of water and a glass which she held out to the soldier.

"I hate Yankees," she said, head high and voice firm, "but I like Mary."

The soldier drained the glass twice, then mounted his horse. He raised his hand in military salute. "Thank you for Mary," he said. Then turning, he gave a quick command to his men, and the company rode away. At the gate he paused to wave his hand.

All day, at intervals, groups of dusty, blue-coated soldiers plodded by. Sometimes companies stopped at the well house, then resumed their weary march; caissons lumbered along drawn by mules; a group of artillery clattered past. Once Sue heard the far-off sound of cannon, and her heart contracted as she thought of Tom. Then she said, "I hope nothing will happen to Mary's brother."

At last all the troops seemed to have passed. Sue, who through the day had thought often of Alida Grant, sought Miss Cecilia, and said:

"If you don't mind, Aunty, I'm going to take Uncle Eph and ride up to Miss Alida's."

"Oh, my dear! I'm afraid it isn't safe, with all these Yankees around," answered Miss Cecilia, anxiously.

"The Yankees have all gone long ago, Aunty," coaxed Sue. "None of them would climb way up there, anyway. I feel as if I must see Miss Alida. Please, Aunty!"

And before the eager pleading, Miss Cecilia reluctantly consented.

An hour later, Sue and the old Negro drew rein before the little garden plot. As Sue glanced at the yard, she gave a cry, then sprang from her horse. Something was clearly wrong. The palings were broken and the flower beds trampled. Throwing the reins to Ephraim, she ran up the path and pushed open the door.

In the usually spotless room, disorder reigned. The rugs were disarranged and soiled with marks of muddy feet, chairs were overturned, a skillet lay broken on the hearth. In the chair by the window sat Alida Grant, her hands clasped tightly. She was staring rigidly before her.

Sue ran to her. "What is it, Miss Alida?" she cried. "Oh, what is it?"

Alida turned slowly toward the corner. Her face worked painfully. Sue followed her gaze—then broke into indignant speech:

"They've taken the coverlid!"

Slow tears rolled down Miss Alida's wrinkled cheeks. "It was a Union man that took it. That's what hurts the most. Not but what I'd give the coverlid and all if it would help any; but when I tried to tell him how it was, he only laughed."

"The coward!" cried Sue. Then, with sudden resolution, she threw her arms around Alida's neck. "Don't you fret, Miss Alida. I'll get the coverlid!"

Before Alida Grant could utter a word of protest, Sue was out of the house and into the saddle. Sue rode rapidly down the mountainside till she reached the main road; then she turned abruptly to the right.

Uncle Ephraim rode up. "Whar you gwine, Miss Sue?" he demanded. "Dis road leads to de Yankee camp."

"That's where we're going," said Sue.

The old Negro looked at her in undisguised dismay. "'Tain't safe, Miss Sue!" he expostulated. "Whatever'll Miss Cely say?"

"You hush, Uncle Ephraim. I'm going to get Miss Alida's coverlid." Sue's cheeks were flushed and her eyes flashing. "If you don't want to go, I'll go alone." And she urged on Dixie.

"Hi-yi!" came a familiar voice from behind.

Sue turned as Negro Ben came riding up.

"Miss Cely done sent me to meet you-all," he explained.

"You're just in time," said Sue, in a relieved tone. "You tell Miss Cecilia that Uncle Ephraim and I have gone to the Yankee camp for Miss Alida's coverlid, and tell her not to worry."

Without more ado, Sue cantered on, leaving Ben staring in openmouthed astonishment. Ephraim followed her doggedly. Through the heat and dust of the summer afternoon they rode. They passed group after group of infantry trudging in the same direction. An occasional band of cavalry went by them. Though many glanced curiously at the two, nobody molested them.

Twilight was already deepening when, from a rise of ground, they saw before them the campfires of a bivouacked army. The evening breeze brought them the distant hum of voices.

Now that her goal was in view, it seemed to Sue that she could never gather courage to carry out her purpose. Her heart beat rapidly. Then there rose before her Alida Grant's face as she had last seen it, and she started down the slope.

Halfway down the hill, the horse swerved sharply.

"Halt! Who goes?" rang out a voice, and from the shadows a sentry stepped, laying his hand on Dixie's bridle. Uncle Ephraim rode quickly to Sue's side.

Sue leaned from the saddle. "I want to see the commander," she said earnestly. "It's important."

The man looked up wonderingly at the young girl. He hesitated, then his hand dropped. "Pass," he said. "Ride straight ahead. Headquarters is in the tent with the flag. You can't miss it."

By the dim light of a lantern swung from the tent pole, Colonel John Wainwright was dictating certain orders to Lieutenant James Warren when an orderly entered. He saluted.

"A messenger for the colonel. Important business."

"Show him in," said the colonel, briefly.

There was a curious expression on the orderly's face as he held back the tent flap. The colonel looked up, then sprang quickly to his feet. Before him stood a young girl in a dusty riding habit, with a Confederate cap on her dark hair. A white-haired old Negro stood behind her.

"How can I serve you?" began the colonel; but the girl was gazing not at him, but at the lieutenant.

"It's Mary's brother!" "And what are you doing here?" they cried simultaneously.

Then, recovering himself, the lieutenant turned to the colonel. "Colonel Wainwright," he said, "permit me to present to you Miss Sue—"

"My name is Susan Howard," said Sue, with dignity, "and I have come to get Miss Alida's coverlid."

"Miss Alida's coverlid!" ejaculated the colonel. He turned an inquiring gaze on the lieutenant, but Warren shook his head.

Then, briefly, Sue told her story. As he listened, the colonel's face was grave, but when at last he spoke, there was a humorous twinkle in his eyes. He glanced significantly at the gray cap.

"I see you're a little Rebel," he said.

"Yes, I am a little Rebel, sir," answered Sue, sturdily; "but won't you please help me to find Miss Alida's coverlid?"

"Who ever let you come here on such an errand?" demanded the officer.

"Nobody let me come," said Sue. "Uncle Ephraim tried to stop me, but I just had to come or it would have been too late. But won't you please hurry, sir? I'm afraid Aunt Cecilia is pretty worried."

The colonel turned to Warren. "Lieutenant Warren, I

appoint you escort to the enemy. If Alida's coverlid is in this camp, find it. If any soldier has it in his possession, put him under arrest at once."

The colonel's voice was very stern. "Cowardly trick!" he said. "And see also," he added, "that Miss Sue has proper escort to her home."

He held out his hand to Sue. "Good luck, little Rebel!" he said smiling.

"Thank you, sir," said Sue. Her dark eyes were grateful.

Warren having summoned an orderly, the search began. From tent to tent, from group to group they went, but not a trace of the coverlid appeared. Nearly the entire camp had been traversed. Sue's eyes ached with looking, and a lump rose in her throat. Always before her she saw Miss Alida's face. "I must find it, oh, I must!" she whispered.

She was startled by Uncle Ephraim's excited voice. "What's dat ober dar, Miss Sue, dar by de ribber?"

Sue looked in the direction indicated. A group of men were gathered about a campfire whose wavering light was reflected in the stream. In the background, stretched between two saplings and serving as a screen, she caught a glimpse of blue and scarlet. Forgetting everything else, she ran forward.

A thickset, coarse-faced man was concluding some story. "And you ought to have seen the old girl's face when I grabbed the blanket!" He laughed boisterously.

All at once he found himself confronted by a dark-haired fury of a little girl in a gray Confederate cap. She gathered the coverlid in her arms, then turned to the astonished soldier. Her dark eyes were flashing.

"It was a cowardly trick!" she cried.

The soldier sprang angrily to his feet, but he found himself looking into the gray eyes of Lieutenant James Warren, whose right hand held a cocked pistol.

"So you're the coward who goes about robbing defenseless old women." Warren's tone was contemptuous. "It's men like you who bring disgrace upon the army." He turned to the soldier accompanying him.

"Purvis, conduct this man to the guardhouse. His case will be settled later."

With an evil glance at the group, the man slouched off under guard.

Unfastening the coverlid, Warren folded it carefully and placed it in Sue's arms.

"Take it to Miss Alida," he said. "And now I think we had better be starting. The sooner you get home, the better."

"Oh, you mustn't come!" cried Sue. "You have been riding all day and you look so tired. I don't mind a bit. Uncle Ephraim will look after me, and besides, I'm so happy!" Sue clasped the coverlid close, her eyes shining.

But when she and Uncle Ephraim rode out of the camp, Lieutenant Warren and his orderly rode with them.

"Poor Aunt Cecilia!" said Sue. "I suppose she's awfully worried, but she won't mind when she knows." Sue patted the coverlid on the saddlebow. "Oh me, I'm glad, glad, glad!"

They soon branched from the main road and were riding up the mountain. Another turn, and the cabin would be in sight. They were passing through a clearing where the moonlight sifted through the branches, when suddenly from the underbrush a shot rang out. Instantly the lieutenant urged his horse between Sue and the thicket. Even as he did so, a second shot was heard. The soldier swayed, then straightened himself.

"Low in your saddles," he commanded. "Now—ride!"

Up the mountain flew the little company. Evidently the shot had been the work of some straggling soldier, some night prowler, for there was no other report.

Now the gleam from the cabin was visible. At the gate, Sue sprang from the saddle without waiting for help. Strangely enough, in the midst of danger she had felt no fear. Now her heart swelled in anticipation of Alida's joy.

She turned to speak to the others. She was just in time to see the lieutenant sink forward on his horse's neck. The orderly and Uncle Ephraim hastened to his side.

"We'll have to get him into the cabin right away," said the soldier, anxiously.

Sue flew up the path and pushed open the door. The cabin had been restored to the usual immaculate order. Alida Grant sat gazing sadly into the dying embers. At the sound of the opening door, she rose quickly; but at the sight of Sue, the look of apprehension faded from her face. Then her eyes fell on the coverlid, and her arms opened involuntarily.

The child ran to her, thrusting the coverlid into those waiting arms. "Here's the coverlid, dear Miss Alida; but they've shot Mary's brother." Sue's face was white.

Already the soldier and Uncle Ephraim were bringing in the lieutenant. His eyes were closed, his face was pallid, and on the shoulder of the blue blouse a spot was widening ominously.

"Lay him down there." She pointed to the bed. "Get off his boots and his blouse. Ephraim, heat water; the pail's in the corner. Sue, bring that roll of linen you'll find in the bottom drawer."

With deft, tender fingers, she worked over the wounded man.

"Bullet went clean through the shoulder," said the orderly, with a sigh of relief. "Good thing it wasn't an inch lower!"

Carefully Miss Alida bathed the wound, binding it up with the soft linen. "That will do till we can get a doctor up here."

With careful hands, she spread the cherished coverlid over the wounded soldier. Her gaunt face had a strangely illuminated look. At last she was doing something for the cause she held so dear.

Slowly the soldier's eyes opened. For a moment he stared blankly, then his gaze fell upon Sue.

"Brave little enemy!" he whispered. He smiled faintly, then his eyes closed again.

"Is he going to get well?" asked Sue, anxiously.

"Of course he's going to get well," said the orderly, reassuringly. "We couldn't spare the lieutenant yet awhile."

Reaction having come, Sue, with her head on Alida Grant's shoulder, sobbed out her heart. Alida's rough fingers stroked the soft hair tenderly.

"I reckon the coverlid's twice as dear to me now," she said.

Still through the summer days the troops in gray moved northward, followed relentlessly by those in blue. Then at last to Sue and Miss Cecilia, anxiously waiting, came the tidings of Gettysburg—tidings softened only by the knowledge that Tom had passed unscathed through Pickett's heroic, but fruitless, charge.

In the cabin on the mountainside, there was rejoicing, saddened by the realization of what the victory had cost.

"It's the beginning of the end," said the lieutenant. "They can't hold out much longer. And I had to miss it!" he added regretfully.

The reason for his missing it brought to mind Sue Howard. "Poor little enemy!" he said pityingly. "This will be hard news for her, Aunty." And Miss Alida nodded sorrowfully.

Tenderly cared for, the wounded man was slowly gaining strength. From the plantation, sent by Miss Cecilia, had come Negro Ben, only to be relegated by Alida to the position of hewer of wood and drawer of water. No hands but hers should touch her soldier.

Almost daily came Sue to read to Mary's brother or to write the letters which he dictated to the folks at home. Sometimes she herself added a postscript to Mary. Often the lieutenant rehearsed to Alida the story of Sue's visit to camp.

"I'll never forget the sight of the colonel's face as he saw the messenger, nor the dignity with which she demanded the coverlid. I fairly shook in my cavalry boots."

Sue only smiled at the teasing. "The colonel was a dear —that is, for a Yankee," she qualified.

"Anyway," continued the lieutenant, "I knew I *had* to find that coverlid; but I little thought that I would be lying beneath it so many weeks."

His hand touched it lightly, then he sighed a little. The soldier found the forced inaction hard.

Miss Alida spoke. "When I think of that child's riding to camp and about your being wounded, all for me, it seems that my heart's too full for words; but I reckon you-all know how I feel. And it does seem to me as if the coverlid was never so beautiful."

At last came the day when the soldier was able to ride away to rejoin his regiment. Alida and Sue stood at the gate to bid him farewell.

"I'll never forget all your kindness, Aunty," he said, and

bending, he kissed her cheek. Miss Alida flushed like a girl.

The soldier raised Sue's hand to his lips.

"Good-by, little enemy," he said, smiling. "Take good care of the coverlid."

Then from his pocket he took the little case containing Mary's picture and handed it to Sue.

"This is a reminder that sometime I'm coming back," he said gravely. "Don't forget me."

Sue's face beamed as she took the picture. "I'll just love it," she said. "When you do come back, bring Mary. I feel that I know her well already."

At something in the soldier's eyes as they rested on the young girl, Alida Grant smiled quietly.

Long years have passed since those summer days. More than half a century ago the coverlid was given to my grandmother as a wedding present from Alida Grant. The actors in the little drama have long since passed "beneath that low green tent, whose curtain never outward swings," but the coverlid still lies along the back of the old davenport, and with the passing years it seems to gather beauty.

For the Honor of the Company

BY MARY E. MITCHELL

The old man came slowly up the little graveled path which bisected the plot, and painfully bent himself to one of the ornate iron settees facing the monument. Everything about him, the faded blue suit, the brass-buttoned coat with the tiny flag pinned on its breast, the old army hat, all bespoke the veteran. He wore, also, a look of unwonted tidiness which sat stiffly on his shambling figure. The frayed edges of his clean linen had been clipped, and his thin gray hair neatly brushed. His whole aspect told of a conscientious concession to the solemn rites of Decoration Day.

The bench already held one occupant, small and withered in person, with soft white hair showing beneath a rusty, old-fashioned bonnet. An observer would have pronounced her a contemporary of the newcomer. But it is harder to tell a woman's age than a man's; the way of her life marks her face more than do the years. In this case her deep corrugations bore witness to stress, but behind the furrows lay something which hinted that the owner had overlived the storms, and that the end was peace.

The little green park which they had chosen for their resting place was a fitting spot for old people, for it, too, spoke of battles past and victories won. The monument was one of those misguided efforts by which a grateful community is wont to show its appreciation of heroic service. It rose from the surrounding sward with a dignity of purpose and a pathos of intention quite worthy of better expression. The scrap of ground around it had been promoted from unkempt waste, trampled by children and the occasional cow, to a proud position of national use. On this particular day it fulfilled its duties with an air of special integrity, while the monument fluttered with decorous gayety in a loyal drapery of red, white, and blue.

The Memorial Day sun was warmly manifesting its patriotism, and the veteran sank into the shaded seat with a sigh of tired content. He took off his hat and mopped his forehead. His part in the program was over, and he had earned his rest. The celebration had been a success; not a threatening cloud had distracted the attention of the audience from the orator of the day. The procession had made an impressive progress to the cemetery, and one more chaplet had been laid upon the grave of the Civil War.

When he had restored his hat to his grizzled head, the veteran straightened up and regarded his seat mate. He was a social soul, and the little cough he gave found no excuse in his bronchial regions; it was a purely voluntary and tentative approach to conversation. The look the woman vouchsafed him did not discourage his advance.

"Sightly place?" he ventured.

"Yes," replied the woman.

"That monument now; it's somethin' to be proud of, ain't it?"

"It's real handsome."

"I ain't been here since it was set up. I belong over Hilton way, but this year the whole county's celebratin' together, you know, an' I thought I'd like to see the boys' names cut up there."

The woman's gaze followed the veteran's to the tablet on the side of the shaft.

"They look good, don't they?" she said softly. "I brought Danny to see them. His gran'father was my husband, an' I give him to his country."

The veteran put his hand to his hat in an awkward gesture of sympathy.

"Well, ma'am," he said, "I often wonder why I warn't taken instead of some better man. I fought right through an' got nothin' but a flesh wound. Lord, but it was the women that suffered; they're the ones that ought to get pensions. I sense as if it was yesterday the mornin' I said good-by to my sweetheart."

For a moment the only sound was that of the breeze gently stirring the fresh young maple leaves overhead. Then the woman spoke.

"It seems queer, don't it, for us to be settin' here, an' them never knowin' that we're proud of 'em, an' that the country they died for is doin' 'em honor all over its length and breadth? If they could come back and join in the procession it would make a long line, but, my, wouldn't we make of 'em! I can't help thinkin' how much more they did than just fight."

"That's so," responded the veteran. "There's somebody that says that when you pass out, what you've done don't die, but goes on livin' on after you, an' I guess he's right. If we sensed that all the time we'd be more careful, mebbe."

"It *has* lived after them," approved the woman. "I feel just that way when I'm thinkin' about my husband. He helped break the chains of the slave, but that warn't all or even most of what he done. I guess the war wouldn't have been lost if he hadn't been in it, but he gave the folks that knew him an example of what bein' a hero is, an' you can't calculate what that's meant."

The veteran nodded.

"I never thought of it just that way before, but I guess you're right, ma'am."

"You take Danny, now; he's the only gran'child I've got, an' we set store by him. Well, he's lame, an' the doctor says he won't ever be better. Seems as if it would fair kill his father when he heard that; men take such things hard, you know, and Danny was his eye's apple. But I guess he had some of the fightin' blood in him, for he marched straight up to the sorrer an' looked it square in the face. 'My father faced the music, an' I guess I won't shame him, though it's a different kind of a bullet that's struck me; one you've got to live with instead of die of,' he told Hatty Anne; she's his wife, an' she told me. As for Danny, well, when he was a little mite with a backache a good deal bigger'n he was, he wouldn't cry out because his gran'father was a soldier. We talk to him a lot about it, an' I guess it's given him courage to live."

"Perhaps the little feller'll get over it," said the veteran sympathetically. "Doctors don't know everything."

The woman shook her head.

"There ain't any perhaps about a spine as crooked as Danny's. But he's real sunny dispositioned an' he's got lots of grit. He's just set on playin' soldier, an' it would make you cry to see him drillin', brave as the best, with his poor little back, an' his pipestem legs. He's over there now, waiting for the band to come back; he's just crazy over bands, Danny is."

The veteran strained his dim eyes in the direction of the little figure sitting, crutches by his side, on the broad curb which swept about the curve of the grassplot.

"My husband didn't leave much in the way of worldly goods," continued the woman, "but I guess the legacy he did leave has gone further an' done more'n dollars would have done."

"That's so! That's so!" affirmed the veteran; and again on the two old people fell silence. It was the veteran who broke it.

"I'm thinkin', as I set here, how the real heroes, an' them that ain't heroes, are all mixed up in a war, an' both get equal credit. Here's your husband, now, a brave man who died for his country, an' then again I could tell you a story—but there! My son's wife says my tongue's longer'n the moral law. I guess when I get goin' I don't know when to stop."

The woman's face expanded in interest as she edged nearer her seat mate.

"I'll be real pleased to hear it," she said.

The veteran painfully crossed his stiff legs, took off his hat and put it on his knee, while with one wrinkled hand he nervously fingered the brim.

"It seems good to be talkin' of old times." The veteran's voice took on an apologetic note. "Young folks don't always know what that means to the old, an' sometimes they get a bit impatient. You can't blame 'em. But this thing I've mentioned I never told but just to one, an' that was my wife; she's dead, now, this twenty year. It ain't a pretty story to tell, or for a woman to hear, but somehow I kind o' feel as if you'd understand. I've never been quite sure I done right; my wife, she thought I did, but you know wives have a way of favorin' what their men do. Perhaps you'll judge different."

The veteran's eyes were fixed on the monument. The woman adjusted herself in an attitude of attention. Now and then there floated over to them the broken sounds of a happy little tune Danny was singing to himself.

"It happened at Gettysburg," said the veteran, "on the second day of the fight. You can't know just how a soldier feels when a battle is in the air. War brings out all that's good in a man, an' right along beside it all that's bad. The thought of the cause you're fightin' for, an' the music, an' the marchin', an' the colors flyin', an' the officers cheerin' the men, all gets hold of somethin' inside of you, an' you could give up everythin' for your country. It's grand, but, Lord, it's no use talkin' about it! You can't put it into words. Queer, ain't it, how many things words can spoil?"

The veteran paused as the woman gave the expected note of assent.

"As for the other side—well, when you're really on the fightin' ground with the bullets flyin' all about you, an' you see the men you've marched with, shoulder to shoulder, shot down, an' you know it's goin' to keep on till one side has to cry quit, then the beast that's in you gets up an' roars, an' you want to kill an' kill; sometimes you turn

sick an' want to run—but you don't; no, ma'am! Runnin'
is the last thing you do. It takes all kinds of feelin's to
make a battle. It's a queer sort of a way to settle troubles,
now, ain't it? Seems kind o' heathenish, don't it?"

The woman shook her head.

"I take it we ain't to criticize what the Lord's sanc-
tioned," she said. "The 'God of Battles' is one of his names."

"Oh, when it comes to the Lord, I ain't takin' exceptions,
of course," responded the veteran with a slightly embar-
rassed air. "I wouldn't set myself up to judgin' His doin's,
but I shouldn't have thought of introducin' war as a
pacifier of nations, myself, or of fightin' as a way to
brotherly love. But then I ain't pious. There's a pretty side
to war, but it warn't showin' itself that day at Gettysburg.

"It was a gloomy mornin', with a mist like a steam
bath, dreary an' drippin'. We couldn't get a sight of anything, an' the fog got into the men's hearts an' wilted them
down, like it does starch out of a collar band. There were
other reasons for feelin' low. Things looked pretty bad for
our side, and every one of us knew it. Our little cap'n
danced about for all the world like a war horse; just a
bundle of nerves. He said a little speech to us . . . *Said!*
It shot right out of him. It hit, too, for the whole company
straightened up as if it had got a backbone. 'You do your
damnedest!' he yelled, 'or by George, I'll shoot every man
of you!' You'll have to excuse me, ma'am; I had to repeat
it just as he said it, or you wouldn't have understood how
wrought up he was; an' 'by George' ain't exactly the
words, either."

The woman nodded indulgently. Her interest outran the
amenities.

"Time dragged that mornin'," the veteran went on.
"After a while the sun burned off the fog, an' everythin' lay

as bright as if there was goin' to be a strawberry festival instead of a bloody battle. The fields was as green as grass an' crops could make 'em, an' the cattle grazed as peaceful as lambs on a May mornin'. One herd of them cows got a taste of what war was before the day was over. It was brought home to them personal, you might say.

"You could hear the cocks crowin' first in one barnyard an' then in another, an' birds was singin' everywheres. Little puffs of far-off smoke was all that told of battle in the air. The mornin' wore on, an' still we waited; there ain't anythin' more wearin' to a soldier's nerves than waitin'. I'd rather fight a dozen battles than spend another mornin' like that.

"It was well on to the middle of the afternoon when the orders was given. There was a racket then, all right! The pretty, peaceful farmyard scene was broke up, an' instead, there was a hell of roarin' guns an' screamin' shells an' blindin' smoke. Talk about slaughter! You've heard of the Devil's Den, I'm thinkin'?"

The woman shook her head.

"It got pretty famous that day. It was a heap of rocks, full of little caves, an' every one of the holes held a Johnny with a sharpshooter. Our men got picked off as fast as they came up. A little ravine ran right by the place, an' the herd of cows I mentioned got penned up right in the range of the crossfirin'. Them animals would have learned a lesson that day, if there'd been anything left of them to remember it with. That's generally the way with life, most of us get our experience too late.

"There was a hill called Little Round Top, an' General Warren see right off that was the key to the situation. There didn't seem to be anybody occupyin' it, but it was such a good point, right on the face of it, that he kep' a sharp eye on it. All of a sudden there came a bright flash from near the top, a blindin' flash that made us sit up an' take notice. The truth of it was a company of Rebs were in ambush, an' the sun struck on to their bayonets an' gave them away complete. It's funny how weather steps in sometimes an' balks things. Seems as if it had more to do with winnin' the battle than the whole army did."

"The ways the Lord takes are beyond the understandin' of man," said the woman. "His arm is ever with the righteous."

The veteran meditatively rubbed his rough hand over his shabbily clad knee, as he remarked:

"Mebbe I don't give the Lord credit where it's due. It seems to me we're mighty apt to call it the Lord's arm when it's on our side. I notice them that lose ain't apt to regard it in that light. However, whoever had the managin' of it, that flash saved the day. Our company was one of those sent up to take the hill. In all the war there warn't a finer charge. I don't see how we ever done it with them guns. It was a steep slope, rocky, and rough with tangled undergrowth. We never could have got up in cold blood. We were facin' a hot fire, but our only thought was to get to the top. There warn't a man in the company but would rather have been shot than face our little cap'n after havin' played the coward. I say there warn't a man—there was one, as I found out, but then, Lord, I don't call that thing a *man*.

"Well, up we went, rattlety bang, yankin' them guns over the rocks, stumblin', scramblin', tearin' our faces an' hands an' barkin' our shins, but keepin' right on. An' that ain't mentionin' the bullets whizzin' all about us."

"It must have been awful," interrupted the woman. "It

takes a lot of prayin' to keep up courage in the face of danger like that."

"*Prayin'!*" ejaculated the veteran. "If you call it prayin' to be bound to keep on if you had to kill every all-fired Reb in the Confederate Army to do it, an' to make a road of their dead bodies, then we was all prayin'. I guess men do things different from women. It don't make any odds what we thought; we *did*, and that was more to the point.

"About halfway up the hill, one of the guns got stuck some way, an' I had to stop an' help free it, so I fell behind a bit. As I was hurryin' to ketch up I stumbled on somethin' soft and yieldin'. It was a man, an' he was wearin' the blue. It took me some seconds to sense what it meant, an' then I realized I had run down a skulker, hidin' in the rocks. I just reached out an' hauled him up by the collar of his coat, an' says I, 'What you doin' here?' He was a man from my own company, worse luck. He was tremblin', and his face was white. I shook him just as I would a rat. 'Lemme alone!' he whimpered. 'I was just gettin' my breath!' 'Gettin' your breath!' I yelled. 'You march up that hill as fast as you can go, or you'll get what mean little breath you've got knocked clean out of you, an' it won't be the Rebs that does it either!' With that I give him a kick that sent him flyin' in the right direction. You see, ma'am, I was hot at havin' our company shamed by a thing like that.

"Everybody knows what we did on that hill, an' how our charge saved the day. The names of the officers we lost on Little Round Top are writ up high in the records of the war; an' the men who fought for 'em an' fell with 'em aren't any less heroes, though they may not be in such big print. You can read all about it in any of the histories, but there's just one little story of that day that never got into a book. Nobody knows it but me, an' I saved our company from shame, an' a dead man's name from bein' a byword an' a reproach.

"That evenin', when the firin' had stopped, I was prowlin' around the hillside, lookin' after the wounded and such. I got off the main track of the charge an' blundered about a bit, tryin' to find my way back. I was gettin' a little impatient to know my course, when I saw somethin' black, lyin' on the ground behind a tree. I halted an' got my gun ready; you see, I thought it was a Johnny, skulkin' round to rob the dead. I crept up softly toward the figure. It didn't move. When I got near I see it was a dead body. It was lyin' on its face, an' its heels pointed uphill. Worse'n that, it was wearin' the blue. With my gun as a lever I turned the body over an' looked at the face. It was more because I didn't want to accuse anyone in my thoughts than because I wanted to see who the scamp was, that I turned him over.

"I bent over him to get a good look, an' there, with his white face starin' up at me, lay the man I had kicked uphill that afternoon. He had been shot as he was runnin' away again, shot in the back. That's the biggest disgrace a soldier can earn, I take it. Not an hour before, I'd been braggin' loud about our company, an' there was a man I'd messed with, an' marched with, givin' me the lie as he lay there, the marks of his guilt hittin' me in the face, as it were. It seemed to me as I stood there in the dusk an' stared down at him, as if he was a big, black blot on our fair record, an' as if he marred the glory of the company that had fought so brave. We was the heroes of the day, an' our deed would be in the mouth of every one the country over, an' that rascal spoilt it all. 'Not a man but has done his duty,' our cap'n had said. Oh, well, it ain't any use talkin', but I was mad clean through.

"As I told you, it ain't a pretty thing for you to hear, but I just took aim at that feller's forehead. It's bad enough to shoot a live man, but to send a bullet into a dead face turned up helpless to you—well—it's just plain butchery! But I done it. My shot hit him fair between the eyes. Then I left him."

The veteran paused. The woman's face was turned toward his; both were lost in the interest of the story. The music of the returning band and Danny's shrill little cheers were unheeded. The streamers on the monument fluttered softly, and the shadow of the shaft, lengthening as the sun traveled to the west, fell upon the two old people. Finally the woman spoke.

"It was an awful thing to do. It makes me think of Indians maulin' the bodies they've killed. But I don't know but you was right. It would have been worse for them that loved him to bear a coward's shame. I guess you was right."

"Thank you, ma'am," returned the veteran. "That's the way my wife took it. I'm glad if you can see it in that light. But you mustn't make a mistake about one thing. I warn't thinkin' about that skulker, or them that loved him, when I done what I did. It was for the company I put that bullet into his dead skull, an' I'd do it for the company's sake forty times over—nasty job as it was.

"Of course," he continued, "I'm glad if his family got any comfort out of the thought that he was hit in the front. I never heard anything about him more, I never even heard if he was found, till I just see his name up there, writ in endurin' stone, along with brave men and heroes.

Then the whole thing came back to me as plain as day, an' I felt the goose flesh run over me, as I did when I shot into that coward's forehead. Yes, when I see that name, carved deep, Dan'el P. Ol—"

"Stop!"

The cry cut the name short, as clean as a shot. The veteran stared in amazement. His companion had wheeled about on the bench, and was facing him. Her old eyes were blazing. Her withered cheeks flushed dark red; then the color went out and left the white of ashes.

"Why, ma'am!" stammered the old man. "Why, ma'am! I guess you ain't feelin' well. I oughtn't to have told you such a story. 'Tain't fit for ladies to hear. I guess you'll have to excuse me. You see, that name brought it back so vivid."

"Oh stop!" again cried the woman. Her hands were working nervously and she was trembling from head to foot.

A slow conviction dawned upon the veteran's bewildered brain.

"Why, ma'am!" he exclaimed once more. "I'm right sorry if it was any one you happen to know. I'd never—"

"Hush! For God's sake, hush!" The woman was panting and breathless. "Don't you see the child is comin'?"

The band had vanished and Danny, who had watched the last back around the corner, was hastening to his grandmother as fast as his crutches would allow. His eager little face was shining with its past delight. The woman rose quickly, clutching the back of the settee for support. The veteran struggled to his feet.

"*The child!*" he repeated in confusion. Then a light broke on him. He took a step forward, but the woman put out her poor quavering hands as if to push him away.

There they stood, these two old people, and stared

dumbly into each other's eyes. The woman read in the man's face the horror of his deed, but she saw nothing to help her misery. The veteran's face was as gray and drawn as that of his companion. His act was beyond recall. What he had smitten was more than life.

Then, as Danny came up and clutched his grand-mother's gown, gazing half shyly, half admiringly at the old man in his uniform, the veteran straightened with a martial air. It was as if a call to battle had put new life into long unused muscles. He stretched out a tremulous hand and laid it on the crooked little shoulder. The rapture of being touched by a real soldier overcame the lad's bashfulness, and he smiled up at the old face above him.

"My grandfather fought in the war," he said.

The veteran's voice was grave and steady as he answered.

"Danny," he said, "always be proud of that. When things go hard you just shut your eyes an' think that you're a soldier's boy, an' that your name's his name, an' that he died in battle. Don't ever go back on that, Danny. There ain't any braver thing than a soldier, an' he died in battle."

"He was shot in the forehead. He was the bravest of the brave," said Danny.

The Home-Coming

BY ELSIE SINGMASTER

Parsons knew little of the great wave of protest that swept over the Army of the Potomac when Hooker was replaced by Meade. The sad depression of the North, sick at heart since December, did not move him; he was too thoroughly occupied with his own sensations. He sat alone, when his comrades would leave him alone, brooding, his terror equally independent of victory or defeat. The horror of war appalled him. He tried to reconstruct the reasons for his enlisting, but found it impossible. The war had made of him a stranger to himself. He could scarcely visualize the little farm that he had left, or his mother. Instead of the farm, he saw corpse-strewn fields; instead of his mother, the mutilated bodies of young men. His senses seemed un-

able to respond to any other stimuli than those of war. He
had not been conscious of the odors of the sweet Maryland spring, or of the song of mockingbirds; his nostrils
were full of the smell of blood, his ears of the cries of dying
men.

Worse than the recollection of what he had seen were
the forebodings that filled his soul. In a day—yes, an hour,
for the rumors of coming battle forced themselves to his
unwilling ears—he might be as they. Presently he too
would lie, staring, horrible, under the Maryland sky.

The men in his company came gradually to leave him
to himself. At first they thought no less of him because he
was afraid. They had all been afraid. They discussed their
sensations frankly as they sat round the campfire, or lay
prone on the soft grass of the fields.

"Scared!" laughed the oldest member of the company,
who was speaking chiefly for the encouragement of Parsons, whom he liked. "My knees shook, and my chest caved
in. Every bullet killed me. But by the time I'd been dead
about forty times, I saw the Johnnies, and something hot
got into my throat, and I got over it."

"And weren't you afraid afterwards?" asked Parsons,
trying to make his voice sound natural.

"No, never."

"But I was," confessed another man. His face was
bandaged, and blood oozed through from the wound that
would make him leer like a satyr for the rest of his life. "I
get that way every time. But I get over it. I don't get hot
in my throat, but my skin prickles."

Young Parsons walked slowly away, his legs shaking
visibly beneath him.

Adams turned on his side and watched him.

"Got it bad," he said shortly. Then he lay once more on

his back and spread out his arms. "God, but I'm sick of it! And if Lee's gone into Pennsylvania, and we're to chase him, and Old Joe's put out, the Lord knows what'll become of us. I bet you a pipeful of tobacco, there ain't one of us left by this time next week. I bet you—"

The man with the bandaged face did not answer. Then Adams saw that Parsons had come back and was staring at him.

"Ain't Hooker in command no more?" he asked.

"No; Meade."

"And we're going to Pennsylvania?"

"Guess so." Adams sat upright, the expression of kindly commiseration on his face changed to one of disgust. "Brace up, boy. What's the matter with you?"

Parsons sat down beside him. His face was gray; his blue eyes, looking out from under his little forage cap, closed as though he were swooning.

"I can't stand it," he said thickly. "I can see them all day, and hear them all night, all the groaning—I—"

The old man pulled from his pocket a little bag. It contained his last pipeful of tobacco, the one that he had been betting.

"Take that. You got to get such things out of your head. It won't do. The trouble with you is that ever since you've enlisted, this company's been hanging round the outside. You ain't been in a battle. One battle'll cure you. You got to get over it."

"Yes," repeated the boy. "I got to get over it."

He lay down beside Adams, panting. The moon, which would be full in a few days, had risen; the sounds of the vast army were all about them—the click of tin basin against tin basin, the stamping of horses, the oaths and laughter of men. Some even sang. The boy, when he heard them, said, "Oh, God!" It was his one exclamation. It had broken from his lips a thousand times, not as a prayer or as an imprecation, but as a mixture of both. It seemed the one word that could represent the indescribable confusion of his mind. He said again, "Oh, God! Oh, God!"

It was not until two days later, when they had been for hours on the march, that he realized that they were approaching the little Pennsylvania town where he lived. He had been marching almost blindly, his eyes nearly closed, still contemplating his own misery and fear. He could not discuss with his comrades the next day's prospects, he did not know enough about the situation to speculate. Adams's hope that there would be a battle brought to his lips the familiar "Oh, God!" He had begun to think of suicide.

It was almost dark once more when they stumbled into a little town. Its streets, washed by rains, had been churned to thick red mud by thousands of feet and wheels. The mud clung to Parsons' worn shoes; it seemed to his half-crazy mind like blood. Then, suddenly, his gun dropped with a wild clatter to the ground.

"It's Taneytown!" he called wildly. "It's Taneytown."

Adams turned upon him irritably. He was almost too tired to move.

"What if it is Taneytown?" he thundered. "Pick up your gun, you young fool."

"But it's only ten miles from home!"

The shoulder of the man behind him sent Parsons sprawling. He gathered himself up and leaped into his place by Adams's side. His step was light.

"Ten miles from home! We're only ten miles from home!" He said it as though the evil spirits which had beset him had been exorcised. He saw the little whitewashed farm-house, the yellowing wheat fields beside it; he saw his mother working in the garden, he heard her calling.

Presently he began to look furtively about him. If he could only get away, if he could get home, they could never find him. There were many places where he could hide, holes and caverns in the steep, rough slopes of Big Round Top, at whose foot stood his mother's little house. They could never find him. He began to speak to Adams tremulously.

"When do you think we'll camp?"

Adams answered him sharply.

"Not tonight. Don't try any running-away business, boy. 'Tain't worth while. They'll shoot you. Then you'll be food for crows."

The boy moistened his parched lips.

"I didn't say anything about running away," he muttered. But hope died in his eyes.

It did not revive when, a little later, they camped in the fields, trampling the wheat ready for harvest, crushing down the corn already waist high, devouring their rations like wolves, then falling asleep almost on their feet.

Well indeed might they sleep heavily, dully, undisturbed by cry or picket or gallop of returning scout. The flat country lay clear and bright in the moonlight; to the northwest they could almost see the low cone of Big Round Top, to which none then gave a thought, not even Parsons himself, who lay with his tanned face turned up toward the sky. Once his sunken eyes opened, but he did not remember that now, if ever, he must steal away, over his sleeping comrades, past the picket line, and up the long red road toward home. He thought of home no more, nor of fear; he lay like a dead man.

It was a marvelous moonlit night. All was still as though round Gettysburg lay no vast armies, seventy thousand Southerners to the north, eighty-five thousand Northerners to the south. They lay or moved quietly, like great octopi, stretching out, now and then, grim tentacles, which touched or searched vainly. They knew nothing of the quiet, academic town, lying in its peaceful valley away from the world for which it cared little. Mere chance decreed that on the morrow its name should stand beside Waterloo.

Parsons whimpered the next morning when he heard the sound of guns. He knew what would follow. In a few hours the firing would cease; then they would march, wildly seeking an enemy that seemed to have vanished, or covering the retreat of their own men; and there would be once more all the ghastly sounds and cries. But the day passed, and they were still in the red fields.

It was night when they began to march once more. All day the sounds of firing had echoed faintly from the north, bringing fierce rage to the hearts of some, fear to others, and dread unspeakable to Parsons. He did not know how the day passed. He heard the guns, he caught glimpses now and then of messengers galloping to headquarters; he sat with bent head and staring eyes. Late in the afternoon the firing ceased, and he said over and over again, "Oh, God, don't let us go that way! Oh, God, don't let us go that way!" He did not realize that the noise came from the direction of Gettysburg, he did not comprehend that "that way" meant home, he felt no anxiety for the safety of his mother; he knew only that, if he saw another dead or dying man, he himself would die. Nor would his death be simply a growing unconsciousness; he would suffer in his body all the agony of the wounds upon which he looked.

The great octopus of which he was a part did not feel in the least the spark of resistance in him, one of the smallest of the particles that made up its vast body. When the moon had risen, he was drawn in toward the centre with the great tentacle to which he belonged. The octopus suffered; other vast arms were bleeding and almost severed. It seemed to shudder with foreboding for the morrow.

Round Top grew clear before them as they marched. The night was blessedly cool and bright, and they went as though by day, but fearfully, each man's ears strained to hear. It was like marching into the crater of a volcano which, only that afternoon, had been in fierce eruption. It was all the more horrible because now they could see nothing but the clear July night, hear nothing but the soft sounds of summer. There was not even a flag of smoke to warn them.

They caught, now and again, glimpses of men hiding behind hedgerows, then hastening swiftly away.

"Desertin'," said Adams grimly.

"What did you say?" asked Parsons.

He had heard distinctly enough, but he longed for the sound of Adams's voice. When Adams repeated the single word, Parsons did not hear. He clutched Adams by the arm.

"You see that hill, there before us?"

"Yes."

"Gettysburg is over that hill. There's the cemetery. My father's buried there."

Adams looked in under the tall pines. He could see the white stones standing stiffly in the moonlight.

"We're goin' in there," he said. "Keep your nerve up there, boy."

Adams had seen other things beside the white tombstones, things that moved faintly or lay quietly, or gave forth ghastly sounds. He was conscious, by his sense of smell, of the army about him and of the carnage that had been.

Parsons, strangely enough, had neither heard nor smelled. A sudden awe came upon him; the past returned: he remembered his father, his mother's grief at his death, his visits with her to the cemetery. It seemed to him that he was again a boy stealing home from a day's fishing in Rock Creek, a little fearful as he passed the cemetery gate. He touched Adams's arm shyly before he began to sling off his knapsack and to lie down as his comrades were doing all about him.

"That is my father's grave," he whispered.

Then, before the kindly answer sprang from Adams's lips, a gurgle came into Parsons' throat as though he were dying. One of the apparitions that Adams had seen lifted itself from the grass, leaving behind dark stains. The clear moonlight left no detail of the hideous wounds to the imagination.

"Parsons!" cried Adams sharply.

But Parsons had gone, leaping over the graves, bending low by the fences, dashing across an open field, then losing himself in the woodland. For a moment Adams's eyes followed him, then he saw that the cemetery and the outlying fields were black with ten thousand men. It would be easy for Parsons to get away.

"No hope for him," he said shortly, as he set to work to do what he could for the maimed creature at his feet. Dawn, he knew, must be almost at hand; he fancied that the moonlight was paling. He was almost crazy for sleep, sleep that he would need badly enough on the morrow, if he were any prophet of coming events.

Parsons, also, was aware of the tens of thousands of men about him, to him they were dead or dying men. He staggered as he ran, his feet following unconsciously the path that took him home from fishing, along the low ridge, past scattered farmhouses, toward the cone of Round Top. It seemed to him that dead men leaped at him and tried to stop him, and he ran even faster. Once he shrieked, then he crouched in a fence corner and hid. He would have been ludicrous, had the horrors from which he fled been less hideous.

He, too, felt the dawn coming, as he saw his mother's house. He sobbed like a little child, and, no longer keeping to the shade, ran across the open fields. There were no dead men here, thank God! He threw himself frantically at the door, and found it locked. Then he drew from the window the nail that held it down, and crept in. He was ravenously hungry, and his hands made havoc in the familiar cupboard. He laughed as he found cake, and the loved drumsticks of his childhood.

He did not need to slip off his shoes for fear of waking his mother, for the shoes had no soles; but he stooped down and removed them with trembling hands. Then a great peace seemed to come into his soul. He crept on his hands and knees past his mother's door, and climbed to his own little room under the eaves, where, quite simply, as though he were a little boy, and not a man deserting from the army on the eve of a battle, he said his prayers and went to bed.

When he awoke, it was late afternoon. He thought at first that he had been swinging, and had fallen; then he realized that he still lay quietly in his bed. He stretched himself, reveling in the blessed softness, and wondering why he felt as though he had been brayed in a mortar.

Then a roar of sound shut out possibility of thought. The little house shook with it. He covered his ears, but he might as well have spared himself his pains. That sound could never be shut out, neither then, nor for years afterward, from the ears of those who heard it. There were many who would hear no other sound forevermore. The coward began again his whining, "Oh, God! Oh, God!" His nostrils were full of smoke; he could smell already the other ghastly odors that would follow. He lifted himself from his bed, and, hiding his eyes from the window, felt his way down the steep stairway. He meant, God help him, to go and hide his face in his mother's lap. He remembered the soft, cool smoothness of her gingham apron.

Gasping, he staggered into her room. But his mother was not there. The mattress and sheets from her bed had been torn off; one sheet still trailed on the floor. He picked it up and shook it. He was imbecile enough to think she might be beneath it.

"Mother!" he shrieked. "Mother! Mother!" forgetting that even in that little room she could not have heard him. He ran through the house, shouting. Everywhere it was the same—stripped beds, cupboards flung wide, the fringe of torn curtains still hanging. His mother was not there.

His terror drove him finally to the window overlooking the garden. It was here that he most vividly remembered her, bending over her flower beds, training the tender vines, pulling weeds. She must be here. In spite of the snarl of guns, she must be here. But the garden was a waste, the fence was down. He saw only the thick smoke beyond, out of which crept slowly toward him half a dozen men with blackened faces and blood-stained clothes, again his dead men come to life. He saw that they wore his own uniform, but the fact made little impression upon him. Was his

mother dead? Had she been killed yesterday, or had they
taken her away last night or this morning while he slept?
He saw that the men were coming nearer to the house,
creeping slowly on through the thick smoke. He wondered
vaguely whether they were coming for him as they had
come for his mother. Then he saw, also vaguely, on the
left, another group of men, stealing toward him, men who
did not wear his uniform, but who walked as bravely as
his own comrades.

He knew little about tactics, and his brain was too dull
to realize that the little house was the prize they sought.
It was marvelous that it had remained unpossessed so
long, when a tiny rock or a little bush was protection for
which men struggled. The battle had surged that way; the
little house was to become as famous as the Peach Orchard or the Railroad Cut, it was to be the "Parsons
House" in history. Of this Parsons had no idea; he only
knew, as he watched them, that his mother was gone, his
house despoiled.

Then, suddenly, rage seized upon him, driving out fear.
It was not rage with the men in gray, creeping so steadily
upon him—he thought of them as men like himself, only a
thousand times more brave—it was rage with war itself,
which drove women from their homes, which turned young
men into groaning apparitions. And because he felt this
rage, he too must kill. He knelt down before the window,
his gun in his hand. He had carried it absently with him
the night before, and he had twenty rounds of ammunition. He took careful aim: his hand, thanks to his mother's
food and his long sleep, was quite steady; and he pulled
the trigger.

At first, both groups of men halted. The shot had gone

wide. They had seen the puff of smoke, but they had no way of telling whether it was friend or foe who held the little house. There was another puff, and a man in gray fell. The men in blue hastened their steps, even yet half afraid, for the field was broad, and to cross it was madness unless the holders of the house were their own comrades. Another shot went wide, another man in gray dropped, and another, and the men in blue leaped on, yelling. Not until then did Parsons see that there were more than twice as many men in gray as men in blue. The men in gray saw also, and they, too, ran. The little house was worth tremendous risks. Another man bounded into the air and rolled over, blood spurting from his mouth, and the man behind him stumbled over him. There were only twelve now. Then there were eleven. But they came on—they were nearer than the men in blue. Then another fell, and another. It seemed to Parsons that he could go on forever watching them. He smiled grimly at the queer antics that they cut, the strange postures into which they threw themselves. Then another fell, and they wavered and turned. One of the men in blue stopped at the edge of the garden to take deliberate aim, but Parsons, grinning, also leveled his gun once more. He wondered, a little jealously, which of them had killed the man in gray.

The six men, rushing in, would not believe that he was there alone. They looked at him, admiringly, grim, bronzed as they were, the veterans of a dozen battles. They did not think of him for an instant as a boy; his eyes were the eyes of a man who had suffered and who had known the hot pleasures of revenge. It was he who directed them now in fortifying the house, he who saw the first sign of the creeping Confederates making another sally from the left, he who led them into the woods when, reinforced by a hundred of their comrades, they used the little house only as a base toward which to retreat. They had never seen such fierce rage as his. The sun sank behind the Blue Ridge, and he seemed to regret that the day of blood was over. He was not satisfied that they held the little house; he must venture once more into the dark shadows of the woodland.

From there his new-found comrades dragged him helpless. His enemies, powerless against him by day, had waited until he could not see them. His comrades carried him into the house, where they had made a dim light. The smoke of battle seemed to be lifting; there was still sharp firing, but it was silence compared to what had been, peace compared to what would be on the morrow.

They laid him on the floor of the little kitchen, and looked at the wide rent in his neck, and lifted his limp arm, not seeing that a door behind them had opened quietly, and that a woman had come up from the deep cellar beneath the house. There was not a cellar within miles that did not shelter frightened women and children. Parsons' mother, warned to flee, had gone no farther. She appeared now, a ministering angel. In her cellar was food in plenty; there were blankets, bandages, even pillows for bruised and aching heads. Heaven grant that someone would thus care for her boy in the hour of his need!

The men watched Parsons' staring eyes, thinking they saw death. They would not have believed that it was Fear that had returned upon him, their brave captain. They would have said that he never could have been afraid. He put his hand up to his torn throat. His breath came in thick gasps. He muttered again, "Oh, God! Oh, God!"

Then, suddenly, incomprehensibly to the men who did not see the gracious figure behind them, peace ineffable came into his blue eyes.

"Why, *Mother!*" he said softly.

Silent Grow the Guns

BY MACKINLAY KANTOR

It was hard to sleep that night, because the armies muttered too close. A dozen times the boy's mother came from her bed, to find Rover in his scanty shirt, standing by the little north window. He would obey her when she ordered him back to his trundle bed, for she said that good soldiers obeyed orders; and his father had been a good soldier until he was killed at Mechanicsville.

But although Rover would soon fall asleep, his bed seemed all too close to the ground. The ground conveyed every boom and shudder of the gaunt columns that lay round about, every growl and horse-cry. Whenever Rover dreamed, it was of Yankee cavalry roaring past the gate again.

And that would awaken him. . . . There he would be at the window again, his little tousled head framed in deepening dawn.

"Rover?"

"Yes, Mammy."

"Now you come to your bed."

"Mammy, it's nigh daylight, I better stay up now."

She came to him in her long nightgown, heavy gold hair hanging around her slender shoulders, and the hair was polished and metallic even in the half-light. Rover reckoned that probably she was the prettiest woman in the world. He reckoned his mother must look like a fairy princess.

"I can't see no soldiers yet."

She knelt and peered. "Honey, you have me so distressed by lingering at this window. Any moment, a musket— Any moment!"

"Pshaw," he scorned, "they done finished all their shooting, and there ain't scarcely been no shots all night. Not since the damnyankees had the battle out in our road."

The young woman groaned.

"I reckon he was killed, Mammy. The damnyankee captain with the black beard!"

"He was a lieutenant colonel, they said." Again she imagined that she could hear his struggling breath, there on the bloodstained boards of her porch. With water and sand, she had scrubbed it . . .

Rover declared: "But I like that other man, the big one with stripes. He gave us bacon. I reckon he must be a kind man."

She looked to where the bacon was lying beside the fireplace, still wrapped in its grimy cloth. "He gave it to us because he came in for water and bandages, and saw

that all the food we had was corn meal." Her voice—
Rover didn't like her voice when it got that way.

He watched low hills growing softer and browner beyond
the fringe of pines.

"Can I put on my britches, Mammy?"

Before she could answer, they both heard the strange
and frightening approach of hoofbeats. But not in the
rutted road outside; muffled and ominous, they came instead from the field toward the southwest.

The young woman whispered: "Lie down." His heart
hammering, the boy huddled in her arms.

Big feet came up on the cottage porch, and iron fingers
began to tap against the door. "Ma'am!" the whisper
called. "Oh, ma'am!"

Softly, a horse blew through his nose.

"Ma'am—it's Sergeant Meers. The Yankee sergeant.
You remember?"

Rover sat up. "It's him, Mammy! Sure enough—"

Lucia Appleby's hand closed on the old pistol at the
head of her bed. "Who is it?" she cried. "What do you
want?"

"I got something for you, lady. Had to come now, before
the Rebs got to smelling around."

In the thinning gloom, Rover saw that her face was
smoother and less stony. Again she became a fairy princess. "I can't let you in," she said in a low voice. "We're
still abed."

There was silence for a moment. The horse stamped
loudly.

"Well," said that voice outside the door, firm and somehow comforting, even though a Yankee voice, "I'll leave it
on the stoop here. Got to get back before the Johnnies see

me . . . For you and the boy, ma'am. Figured it might come handy."

They heard him crossing the porch, and heard the creak of his stirrup as he mounted. The valley awakened with a single gunshot, and it sounded as if someone had thrown a stone through the porch roof. Hoofs pounded rapidly on the tender sod; another gun banged, but farther away.

"Oh, Mammy, did they shoot him?"

Rover's mother threw a quilt around her shoulders and ran to the porch door. Lifting the bar, she stepped quickly outside and hurried to the end of the low gallery, and Rover ran with her. Through the pink light a horseman was loping easily across Webley's field; he had jumped the fence out of their yard, and now he turned and waved his hand.

The boy caught up a loose grain sack. "Mammy, look! There's a tin can and another bag in it."

At the kitchen table, they examined their gifts. "Flour," Lucia whispered. "Do tell! Wheat flour. Must be five pounds."

He danced beside her, striking the chill out of his bare feet. "What's it say on the big tin can?"

She read: "Turner's Eclipse Sweet Peaches in Brandy."

"Peaches!" He pranced and brayed. "What's brandy?"

"It's a kind of drink."

"Is it good?"

"I don't know, Rover. So long a time—"

"Mammy, do the damnyankees eat this kind of truck every day?"

She gasped, "Oh, yes."

"Mammy, don't cry. Oh, don't cry! . . . I wish that soldier would come back again. Don't you, Mammy? Don't you wish he'd come again?"

"Get on your britches," she ordered sharply, "and then you can go out to the gate—if you'll take good care."

More soldiers might be coming, from one direction or the other. Rover looped the home-sewn galluses over his shoulders, and raced out to swing on the old gate. Two bluebirds flickered along the rail fence across the road. They were dark as swallows in the dawn.

A squad of horsemen toiled up the long hill from the east. Against the fruity colors of the sky, they were coal black and enormous; gradually they grew grayer and grayer, and gray they remained when they had halted in the road and sat looking down at the boy.

Even after two days of it, Rover couldn't forget his disappointment at seeing such thin soldiers as these. It was unethical for soldiers to have their elbows bursting from torn sleeves, and for soldiers to be barefoot. One of them was munching from a handful of cracked dry corn; it was the corn which horses should eat. The man's thin lips curled back with pain, and Rover saw that his gums were raw and bleeding, but still he tried to chew.

"Buddy, was there Yankees hereabouts?" asked one of the men.

"Just one, sir," whispered Rover. "The same one that gave my mammy the bacon. He came again."

Even in laughter, their voices sounded reedy and brittle. "Bacon? There hain't no bacon in the hull world."

They gazed toward the village, searching each grove and hedgerow with shrewdly appraising eyes. "Where's your pappy, bub?"

"He went away when I was little," Rover explained, "and got killed in a war at Mee-cran-icks-ville. I can't recollect what he looked like, but Mammy said he looked powerful like me."

Sun brushed that mountain, miles in the northwest, but here the road hung in shadow. The Rebels grinned down at Rover; their hard-bitten faces were reddened by the freshening light. "What's your name?" asked an old man with a matted short beard. "Ben-Butler-Got-Bit-by-a Bear?" Without waiting for a reply, he ordered: "Too much Yank over yonder. I see their cavalry in the field . . . About—whee! Furrurrd!"

They turned their bony horses and started down the hill. Rover yelled after them. "That ain't my name! It's Roverton Andrews Appleby, but Mammy calls me Rover because I run away!" He saw the oldest soldier reach up his skeleton arm and let a budding elm branch slide through his fingers; thus the soldier gathered a handful of young elm buds, and he stuffed the handful into his mouth, and was chewing as he rode.

The guns began, and interfered with breakfast. Even though you are seven years old, and haven't eaten fried cakes made with white flour since you were five—even so, you cannot enjoy them when three-inch guns are smashing a spring morning to pieces.

"We'll have us a tea party, Rover. We'll sit on the floor."

"I don't want no tea party." His eyes looked as black as any cat's eyes in the night. "I want to watch—"

The little house was frightened, and quivered because of it.

"You can't see. There's nothing to watch! Just smoke. Come now, sit on the floor, like Mammy." She tried to keep that smile nailed upon her face, but the chipped teacup shook in her hand.

"I want to see."

She cried, "Look you here, I've done opened the peaches. See! So big and yellow—kind of like gold. Maybe like pumpkin—"

Far away, immense congregations of men and animals had been turned loose to gallop and yell and halloo at one another. But now something sighed in the air close above this house: there was a wrenching burst of flame and flying dirt in Webley's field.

Lucia clutched the boy so tightly that he yowled. His knee pushed against his plate and sent it teetering over the floor; a trickle of yellowish juice made a lake on the scrubbed boards. "Look," she gasped, "wasted. It's spilled. Just like— What a sight of waste!"

"I'm sorry," he whimpered. "I didn't see that ol' plate."

Lucia told him, "Mammy's not blaming you. Not a mite. I'm thinking about—spilled out for no good reason—"

There was no manner in which he could understand her, so it was best not to worry about it. He wondered about the big Yankee, and where he rode, and if he had been hurt by all these storms.

"Mammy," he asked, "isn't this Sunday?"

She considered. "Yes, Rover." And it seemed their sudden realization was shared by the guns, for the nearer reports began to slacken as if in shame.

But another hour or two had passed before the angry explosions moved entirely beyond the horizon. When the woman and the boy went outside, they found a mat of dun-colored smoke lying above the Tibbs place, and away over northeast toward Sweenys'. In unplumbed distances, gunfire still resounded; nevertheless Lucia knew that she must work in her garden. Sunday or not, whether battles came close or stayed away, she and Rover would need food in the future.

She put aside her breakfast dishes. The peach juice and brandy she poured into a glass jar, and set it on the table.

"I'll take that up to McLeans' as a gift," she explained. "They've been mighty good to us, and I hate always to approach them empty handed. Maybe by afternoon it'll be safe to go."

Rover eyed the golden jar; he said nothing. His toes were tingling with the itch of one who must be up and gone. When entire armies churned the countryside, he couldn't remain hidden forever, as if he were a baby.

"Mind, you stay close," Lucia directed, and then she went out to the kitchen garden, the late morning sunshine on her hair.

He took the jar of juice and crept warily from the front door, and hung behind the berry bushes until he was well out into Webley's field. After all, Mammy wouldn't mind— not a great deal. In fact, it occurred to him that he could go to the McLeans' and back, before ever she missed him. When she discovered that he had delivered the brandy to Mrs. McLean, she might be glad that he had saved her so much trouble.

His conscience lost its last feeble grip as he approached the village. There were no riders blocking the roads; dark-coated men who peered hawklike, watching the river valley and the Sweeny farm. The open sunlight was not so friendly as Rover had hoped it would be. At the McLeans' house, he would feel more comfortable.

Dark-blue strangers prowled near the courthouse, and there were six cannon and more bluecoats beside Ragland's store; but in the southwest there must have been a million. Rover sensed the constant whinnying of horses, and the confused buzzing where uncounted columns lay in wait over toward Nebraska Station. A mushroom of black smoke grew from the spring haze on the horizon; some building was being burned.

A lone soldier roared, "Hey! Boy! Come out of that!" and Rover knew that the man was yelling at him. He began to run, his tough little feet splitting the fresh green tangles, and he ran so fast that his breath tried to burst out of his ears. Then, through the aching fog before his eyes, he saw a red-brick house behind its white fence amid the locust trees, and out in the road was a figure he knew: Mr. Wilmer McLean.

He gulped, "Mammy sent—" as he stumbled down the embankment, and then he pitched headlong amid a crash of glass and a spray of peach juice and brandy.

He lay wailing mournfully.

"Come, come!" Mr. McLean picked him up; he took out a yellow bandana handkerchief and wiped Rover's face. "Cut yourself? No. You ought to be home."

The boy sobbed: "It was brandy and peach likker! Mammy wanted you folks to—"

"You've cut and run again," the farmer deduced severely. "If my young 'uns did that, I'd blister their bottoms."

Down the road, the buzz of voices and hoofs and wheels had become a mounting threat that pushed steadily closer.

Rover whinnied, "But, Mr. McLean, Mammy wanted you-all to have the peach juice, and—"

Now an invasion sprang from the south and whirled around the bend beyond the old slave house. The farmer dragged Roverton Appleby out of the road. Horsemen went careening past without looking to right or left. An officer bawled, "Cut out—squadron—moving behind skirmish line!" and then the herd had crashed past Ragland's store in a splashing spray of half-dried mud.

Mr. McLean wiped specks of clay from his face. "Sonny," he crowed at Rover, "you scoot up in my yard, and don't you go out of it!" He seized the boy by his collar and the seat of his breeches, and swung him across the trodden flower beds.

From under the porch, a pink face was peeping out. The porch was raised on posts the whole width of the house, higher than Rover's head, and underneath was a fine place for dogs to sleep or children to explore.

"Rover!" called a small voice.

The small voice was Nellie's. She was only about six—a generation younger than the mighty Rover. On his hands and knees, he confronted her. "Look-a-here," he scowled, "you go away from under this porch. I don't want no little girl babies around with me." Far away, he heard bugles blowing—several of them, ripping out a chorus of brassy notes.

Nellie giggled. She sat sedately, watching him, her grass-stained petticoats folded primly around her short, plump legs.

"Nellie McLean, you go along!"

"I will not. This is my pa's place, I guess."

"He told *me* to come up here. He—he said for me to stay here all alone, and watch out for damnyankees."

Sunlight pressed down, cool and flat against the vivid green grass of the yard. There were violets all around the porch steps.

Nellie said, "Damnyankees couldn't catch me."

"Yes, they could."

"No, no, no!"

"Well, you just watch. They will."

For a moment she glared at him. But he scowled, and he was bigger and older than she. Nellie's chin began to shake.

"They will not. Pa won't let 'em."

"Reckon he couldn't stop 'em if they come after you. And then they'll"—he took a deep breath—"cook you and *eat you up.*"

Nellie's lower lip curled slowly outward. She blubbered, burying her face in her hands. Far across the fields swept that ever-present grumble of armies, but there didn't seem to be any more shooting. It was dark beneath the porch. Through this stealthy silence enemies might creep up on them.

Rover began to feel rather alarmed, himself. "I reckon I better go," he muttered. He heard horses. "Nellie!" he managed to gasp. She lifted her face, all tear-stained.

"Soldiers coming!"

"I don't want to be et," she wailed.

"*Shhh!*"

They peeped out. The horses had gone past. But the longer Rover thought about it, the more convinced he became that the Yankees were planning, truly, to eat both himself and Nellie. "We better hide," he said, his throat clammy.

"Whereabouts?" Nellie demanded.

"In your house," he whispered.

Eagerly she scrambled to her feet. "Ma and Willie are upstairs. Likely we can play in the back entry. We could have a dolly wedding, maybe!"

He groaned. "I don't want no doll weddings."

Again they heard the ominous mumble; it came from the direction of the courthouse. Before he knew it, Rover was on the front steps, and Nellie clattered behind him. "Wait for me!" she implored.

"You hurry up! Maybe they'll take us to jail and shoot us with pistols!" He dragged her up the tall steps.

The front door was standing ajar, and even the dark hall shadows were more reassuring than the damp regions under the porch. The children scampered inside.

Nellie whispered: "They're coming in the yard—"

Over his shoulder, Rover saw horses' heads and brass buttons and swords glittering in at the gate. That was all he needed to see. "*Where'll we hide?*" burst from his palsied lips; and before she could answer, he had scuttled into the parlor.

"Look out the window, Rover!"

"No!"

She wrung her hands, and jigged up and down.

He took a very small peek, and his eyes bulged. "Your pa's with 'em!" Then she had crept to his side, and together they crushed the muslin curtains. In the yard, men were dismounting; soldiers in blue, and other soldiers in gray. Two of them—"This is your own home, sir?" they heard the younger Rebel ask Mr. McLean.

"Nellie, they're coming inside!"

She gobbled with fear.

"Let's hide."

She trotted behind a little table by the window, and squatted down. "Like this?"

"No! That hain't no good. Here!" He raced across the room and flung himself recklessly beneath the sofa in the farthest corner. There he lay buried in dusty gloom, and he could hear the rapping of his own heart.

Nellie's red-and-blue striped legs came toward the couch; she got down on her stomach and wriggled under.

Her skirts made a lot of noise. "*Shhh!*" Rover hissed, for already heavy feet were climbing the porch stairs outside.

"Will they kill Pa?" she whispered against his ear.

"*Shhh!*" and then the boots were walking into that room.

A man inquired, steadily, "Do you think this satisfactory, Colonel Marshall?"

"Quite satisfactory, sir."

Mr. McLean suggested, "Maybe another room—" His voice was shrill and unsteady; seldom had he ever used that tone before.

"Thank you, sir. But this should serve. We thank you for your kindness." A chair scraped; there was the jingle of spurs, and then the men all sat down—all except Mr. McLean. Rover heard him go tiptoeing away. One of the men had seated himself on the sofa. Springs sagged low above the children, and the boots and sword scabbard were planted directly in front of their eyes.

Part of the time, the men talked about Mexico. One of them kept interrupting nervously, and saying, "Any moment, sir; he should be here any moment. The orderlies must have located him by now—"

Rover dreaded no longer that the soldiers would eat him up, for two of these men were Confederates, unmistakably. The bigger Confederate would protect Roverton Appleby and protect Nellie too. You could tell that he would protect children, merely by looking at his face. He sat at the opposite side of the room, and his uniform was spotless; his buttons shone like jewelry, and he had a gleaming sword beside him. On the little table near his chair lay his hat and gloves; his beard was wintry gray, and Rover imagined that God must have a similar kind of beard.

(*"Yes, Colonel Babcock. That was some time after the*

battle of Chapultepec. General Scott spoke with him, I believe.")

In the distant kitchen, corn bread was being baked. Its smell drifted into the room like sunshine, but none of these soldiers seemed to be thinking of dinner. Maybe Mrs. McLean would let Rover stay and eat with the family, when she discovered that he was there. Once before he had done so, and he had told Lucia about it many times. They had preserves, and white linen napkins, and more milk than Rover had ever drunk before. The McLeans must be mighty rich.

(*"It's the General, sir! And staff—out at the gate. If you will excuse me for a moment, I'll—"*)

Rover hissed softly in Nellie's ear, "Where's your pa? Maybe he went to eat at table." But her round eyes stared closely into his; she said nothing; and then he realized that the presence of these big bearded men had stricken her into silence. If she dared not move or twitch, she dared not whisper. And now a parade of new boots marched into the parlor. Belts squeaked; little chains jingled; men cleared their throats stealthily, as if ashamed to breathe. It sounded like the funeral to which Mammy had taken Rover, after old Mrs. Webley died.

A new voice. The man spoke in a flat tone, with an awkward pause between each phrase.

(*"Surprised indeed, General, that you remember me at all. You were Chief of Staff. I was merely a subordinate artillery officer."*)

The boots got in the way, and made it difficult to see across the room. Sometimes they made a solid forest of shiny, mud-speckled leather, but sometimes they'd open up and let Rover peek between them. A new man, the owner of the new voice, had seated himself in a chair, more nearly in front of the fireplace, and closer to the sofa where the children lay hidden.

He was a short man. He looked shabby and rather sick, and worn by travel, and he didn't have any sword at all. Rover didn't give shucks for this kind of a Yankee. The soldier looked as if he must have had a headache, for he kept rubbing his head while he talked. His uniform was not new; his buttons did not shine like the buttons of the Rebel who had a beard like God.

(*"No, General Lee. I hadn't thought a lot about terms. Just meant that your army should lay down their arms. Not take them up again during the—the continuance of the war. Unless exchanged—"*)

Nellie was asleep. Several times Rover had whispered to her, and once her silky head had moved, but it did not turn in his direction. She lay flat on the floor, as relaxed and motionless as an abandoned rag doll. Now she moaned and twisted round. Now she was facing him, but her eyes were tightly closed, and her lips half open. She sighed in her sleep.

Rover felt bereft. He wished with weary desire that these soldiers would go back to their camps, and would let him crawl from the room, and maybe run home. Lucia Appleby would be wondering what had happened to him; she might think that he had been run over, or shot, and then again she might decide that he had run away again. A dangerous light would glitter in her blue eyes; she'd break a switch from the willow tree, and trim off the leaves. She'd start in search of him; he would be switched, and knowing well that he deserved it.

(*"Ink,"* the voices said. *"Colonel Parker, have you a*

bottle of ink? . . . The manifold order book. . . . No, I'll take it over here at the table.")

Somebody crept along the hall; somebody opened the door. A whisper, and then Mr. McLean gasped shrilly, "Yes sir! I'll fetch some. Yes sir!" and hours afterward a man said, "Here it is."

Rover's father was killed at Mechanicsville, and Rover could not remember what his father looked like. Mammy said he looked much like Rover . . . There was bacon in the sack, and peaches set away in the brown-and-white dish; some day the Yankee would bring them some more peaches; some day Rover himself would be a soldier, and he would kill many Yankees.

"Ink," the officers repeated forever, and Nellie was asleep. Rover could hear her steady breathing. Sometimes her plaid dress rustled slightly when she moved. (*"It's all dried up, sir, sorry to say . . . Thank you, Colonel Marshall."*) A pen squeaked. Someone coughed. In a dreamy haze, Rover gazed through the paling of leather legs, and he saw that the big gray-bearded Rebel had put on his glasses, and was reading something written on yellow paper. Probably God did have a beard like that, only a mighty sight longer.

In the sunny April world outside, the distant guns no longer voiced their thunder. Reckless herds of horsemen were not quaking along the roads; it seemed instead that people stood stock-still amid the locust trees and waited for something to happen. A great many people, and all of them breathing tensely—a deep, reverent breathing as of sleeping hosts. Or perhaps it was only little Nellie McLean's breath, sighing so regularly near Roverton Appleby's ear, and his own breath whistling in response.

("I take it most of your men are small farmers. This whole country's been so badly raided by both armies, I don't see how they can put in a crop without the aid of the horses they're riding now.")

"No," he had told the Rebels. "My name hain't Ben-Butler-Got-Bit-by-a-Bear. It's Roverton Andrews Appleby, but Mammy calls me Rover because I run away."

When the room shuddered with sudden whoops and hurrahs, the children were torn from their sleep. But after a moment both of them knew where they were, even with all the deep-voiced laughter volleying over them.

Nellie blinked owlishly into Rover's eyes. "I hear Pa—"

"Let's sneak out in back of the sofy," he whispered.

Creeping like rats, they backed out from under the big couch, and passed its corner on their hands and knees. No one was looking at them, and they sidled behind two bearded Yankees who were pounding each other on the back; then they had reached the doorway.

The tall, grave-faced Rebel with the glittering sword had gone. All Rebels seemed departed from the face of the world. A dozen blue-bloused officers milled in the parlor; their faces were red, and the house quaked with their laughter.

Mr. McLean was at the door, his cheeks very pale. He stepped backward before the advance of a voluble officer, and nearly fell over his daughter.

"You young 'uns," he yapped at them sharply, "keep out of here! Mind, Nellie! Don't you come in this room."

Rover clutched her hand. "He don't know we *were* in there."

"I'm hungry," she whined. "I'm going out to the kitchen."

He said, "So'm I—mighty hungry. We must have slept

and slept, like 'coons in a tree." He thought of Lucia Appleby, and in his fancy she had a switch in her hand, just as he had dreamed. "But I better go home."

"Twenty dollars, gold," snapped one of the soldiers to Mr. McLean. "For that little table, where Lee had his hat."

Mr. McLean echoed, "Twenty dollars! Well, I—"

The Yankee had a keen, harsh face with a militant jaw. He was burned by sun and wind to a deep brown, and he did look like a man who might cook and eat a boy who didn't keep out of his way. "Very well! Twenty dollars. Gold." Coins chinked in his hand. "Here you are. Sold and got the tin!"

Gold. Nellie had fled away, but Rover edged back against the wall, and stared. People in fairy tales had gold. The Yankee forced his way through the crowd, and came back carrying the little table which had stood near the front window. He stamped past Rover without looking at him.

He called, "Custer! Here. Table where Lee wrote his acceptance. Present this to Mrs. Custer—my compliments."

A young man came rattling up to the door, and seized the table. He had long yellow hair and a black velvet jacket, and the sharpest eyes Rover had ever seen. "She'll be thankful to have it, General Sheridan."

In the parlor, someone else reached out and grasped Mr. McLean's shoulder. "How about the other table, sir?" A man was lifting the clock from the mantelshelf.

It looked as if they were going to take all of the McLeans' furniture with them; they might even decide to take Rover. He squirmed past an incoming tribe, and sped across the porch. The yard was full of horses, and more crowded at the gate. The whole highway was peopled with blue cavalry. Still carrying the little table hoisted across his black velvet shoulder, the yellow-haired young officer had mounted a big horse and was riding rapidly through the press. He gave shrill yelps as he rode, and the soldiers swung their caps and howled back at him.

Rover clambered over the side fence. He could travel across the field behind Ragland's store, and east of the jail, where the Yankees might not gallop over him. He ran as fast as he could, but always he looked toward his left into the little village, and beyond. It appeared that creation was blossoming into Union blue and horses and gray-topped wagons, and the whole of humanity was shrieking aloud.

Distantly, cannon began to slam at regular intervals. *Blom. Blom. Blom. Blom.*

He crept under the rails of Mr. Webley's fence. Last year's grass lay matted, thick and dry; the rough weeds scratched at Rover's bare legs. *Blom. . . .* Then he was rolling head over heels, for something huge lay in his path, and he had fallen over it. He lifted his head, panting, and looked back. A man in tattered butternut coat and pants lay there, staring at the sky. His eyes were like great marbles, and his face was a solid chalky purple, and one shoulder was drenched with a brown stain. *Blom. Blom.* Rover crawled away for a few yards; then he got up and ran like the wind.

His mother was out at the gate, looking this way and that, heedless of the banging of the big guns.

"Rover, Rover!" she cried.

It seemed good to be in her arms again. "I went to sleep at McLeans'," he mumbled.

Blom.

And that was the last. The reports stopped, suddenly.

"They were shooting again, Mammy—"

"Those were salutes being fired. You wicked boy! You ran away." She kept kissing him; her face was damp, and all hot with a fever of worry.

He wriggled. "You said you wanted McLeans to have the peach stuff. I took it, but it got spilt while I was toting it."

She sobbed, "The war— They just told me. The Yankees came past. The war—"

"What?" he wanted to know.

"It— General Lee has surrendered."

"We licked them damnyankees, I reckon," Rover cried, shrilly.

She said, "No. Oh, no! We've lost."

He thought about it as she led him into the house. "Well," he said, "I reckon one of these days we'll lick 'em."

She found that he had eaten nothing at the McLeans' and so she began to build up the fire, while he was washing at the bench in the rear yard. Hoofs crowded along the narrow road, and presently one horse turned in at the gate. When Lucia and Rover went to the front door, they found their Yankee sergeant swinging down from his horse.

"Good afternoon, ma'am," he said, a bit sheepishly. "I got over, soon's I could, to see how you were getting on."

A faint color came into Lucia Appleby's face. "I suppose you've heard—"

"Yes, ma'am." But he said nothing more about it. Instead he was bringing in another grain sack. "Army biscuits. Sorry I couldn't find no decent bread. But I did get some dried apples, and some more bacon."

Rover's mother stood there and looked at him. Her chin came up, sharply. "Why do you do this, sir?"

He scratched his cap bill, and grinned. Rover liked the
way the man's eyes crinkled up when his mouth twisted
under its mustache. "Why, ma'am! You and the boy— So
to speak, nobody to look out for you—and—rations mighty
scarce. I just thought—"

Lucia's eyes fell. Her lips were very red. "I shouldn't
wonder," she said helplessly, "but what you were hungry
yourself."

"Now that you mention it, lady, I— Well, after I was
here this morning I had a snack. Just a snack."

"If you've got time," she said, "I'll cook a bite for you."
She seemed looking beyond him, down a road which
stretched farther than the North Branch of the river,
farther even than Mechanicsville. She whispered, "I'm the
Widow Appleby."

The cavalryman unbuckled his saber belt.

"I'm Meers, ma'am. Joseph Meers, from Bedford, up in
York State. Looks to me like you need some more wood."
He strode through the kitchen. Out at the tiny woodpile
he picked up a broken-handled ax. Rover sat on the old
poplar stump and watched admiringly as the big man
drove the ax blade deep into a chunk of pine.

Then wagons resounded in the road, and Rover hastened to see them pass. They were loaded with boxes and
bags, and they came from the village. All along the fences
beyond the Appleby house, clusters of ragged men stood in
silence, watching as the Federal wagons approached.
"Here you be, Johnny," said a hoarse voice, and the first
box of hardtack was tossed out into the grass. One of the
Confederates waved his thin hand. Then they all gathered
round the box and began to break it open.

The White Feather

BY THOMAS BAILEY ALDRICH

In *The Thousand and One Nights* the vizier's daughter, Scheherazade, told all the stories; but in our single séance the tales were told by five men, gathered round the hearthstone of a New England roadside tavern, in which they had sought shelter from a blizzard and were snowbound for the night. The sleighing party thus circumstanced found themselves, after supper, in a comfortable sitting room with a blazing fire of hemlock logs in front of them, and for lack of more original entertainment, fell to storytelling. Though each of the five narratives which then took shape in the firelight had its own proper *raison d'être*, I shall reproduce only one of them here. The narrative so specialized owes its consequence, such as it is, to the fact that the narrator—nearly a personal stranger to me—was obliged to leave it in a manner unfinished, and that I, by singular chance, was able to supply what might be called a sequel.

This story, which I have named "The White Feather," was related by a Massachusetts veteran of the Civil War, who had left one arm behind him on the field and in the record of his regiment a reputation for great bravery. The Major, as I subsequently learned, had received a military education at a period when the army held out but scant inducements, and had turned aside from it to study law. At the beginning of hostilities in '61, he offered his services to the Federal government, and was placed upon the staff of General ———, with the rank of captain. The grade of major was afterward won in a Massachusetts regiment. Severely wounded at Spottsylvania Courthouse, and permanently disabled, he resigned his commission, and, after a long invalidism, took to the law again.

With the fullest claim to the later title of judge, he prefers to be thought of and addressed as the Major. Today, his sinewy, erect figure and clear blue eyes, gentle and resolute by turns behind their abatis of gray eyebrow, give no hint of his threescore years and ten, especially when he is speaking.

"Some men," began the Major, setting his half-emptied tumbler a little farther back from the edge of the table, "some men have a way of impressing us at sight as persons of indomitable will, or dauntless courage, or sterling integrity—in short, as embodiments of this or that latent quality, although they may have given no evidence whatever of possessing the particular attribute in question. We unhesitatingly assume how they would act under certain imaginable circumstances and conditions. A gesture, a glance of the eye, a something in the intonation of the voice, hypnotizes us, and we at once accept as real what may be only a figment of our own creating. My story, if it's what you would call a story, deals incidentally with one of these curious prepossessions."

The Major paused a moment, and beat a soft tattoo with two fingers on the arm of the chair, as if he were waiting for his thoughts to fall into line.

"At the outbreak of the war, Jefferson Kane was in his senior year at West Point. The smoke of that first gun fired in Charleston harbor had hardly blown away when he withdrew from the Academy—to cast his lot, it was surmised, with that of his native State, as many another Southerner in like circumstances was doing; for Kane belonged to an old Southland family. On the contrary, he applied for service in the army of the North—in the then nebulous Army of the Potomac. Men of his training were sorely needed at the moment, and his application was immediately granted.

"Kane was commissioned first lieutenant and provisionally assigned for duty in a camp of instruction somewhere in Massachusetts, at Readville, if I recollect. There he remained until the early part of '62, doing important work, for the recruits that passed through his hands came out finished soldiers, so far as drill was involved. Then Kane was ordered to the front, and there I fell in with him—a tall, slender young man, with gray eyes and black hair, which he wore rather long, unlike the rest of us, who went closely cropped, Zouave fashion. I ought to say here that though I saw a great deal of him at this time, I am now aware that the impression he produced upon me was somewhat vague. His taking sides with the North presumably gave mortal offense to his family; but he never talked of himself or of the life he had left behind him in the South. Without seeming to do so, he always avoided the topic.

"From the day Kane joined our regiment, which formed part of Stahl's brigade, he was looked upon as a young fellow destined to distinguish himself above the common. It was no ordinary regiment into which he had drifted. Several of the companies comprising it were made up of the flower of New England youth—college seniors, professional men, men of wealth and social rating. But Kane was singled out from the throng, and stood a shining figure.

"I cannot quite define what it was that inspired this instant acceptance of him. Perhaps it was a blending of several things—his judicial coolness, his soldierly carriage, the quiet skill and tact with which he handled men drawn from peaceful pursuits and new to the constraints of discipline; men who a brief space before were persons of consideration in their respective towns and villages, but were now become mere pawns on the great chessboard of war. At times they had to be handled gingerly, for even a pawn will turn. Kane's ready efficiency, and the modesty of it— the modesty that always hitches on to the higher gifts— naturally stimulated confidence in him. His magnetic Southern ways drew friends from right and left. Then he had the prestige of the West Pointer. But allowing for all this, it is not wholly clear what it was that made him, within the space of a month, the favorite of the entire regiment and the idol of Company A, his own company. That was the position he attained with apparently no effort on his part. Company A would have died for him, to a man. Among themselves, round the mess table, they didn't hide their opinion of Jeff Kane, or their views on the situation at large. The chief command would have been his, could the question have been put to vote. 'I wouldn't like to lose the kid out of the company,' observed Sergeant Berwick one day, 'but it would be a blessed good thing if he could change shoulder straps with the colonel.'"

Here the Major suddenly remembered the unfinished bourbon and Apollinaris in his glass and interrupted himself.

"The colonel alluded to by the sergeant was a colonel of politics, and ought to have stuck to his glue factory down East. In those days we had a good many generals and colonels, and things, with political pulls. I think there were more than a few of that kidney in our recent little scrimmage with Spain. I don't believe in putting protégés and hangers-on out of employment over the heads of men who have been trained to the profession of arms. Some fine day we'll be convinced of the expediency of stowing the politicians. We ought to have a National Cold Storage Warehouse on purpose. But that's another story, as our friend Kipling remarks—too frequently."

The Major flicked off a flake of cigar ash from the looped-up empty sleeve that constantly gave him the oratorical air of having one hand thrust into his shirt bosom, and went on with his narrative.

"We were as yet on only the outer edge of that lurid battle summer which no man who lived through it, and still lives, can ever forget. Meanwhile vast preparations were making for another attempt upon Richmond. The inertia of camp life with no enemy within reach tells on the nerves after a while. It appeared to be telling on young Kane's. Like the regiment, which hitherto had done nothing but garrison duty in forts around Washington, he had seen no active service, and was ready for it. He was champing on the bit, as the boys said. His impatience impressed his comrades, in whose estimation he had long since become a hero—with all the heroism purely potential.

"For months the monotony of our existence had been enlivened only by occasional reconnaissances, with no result beyond a stray Minié ball now and then from some outlying sharpshooter. So there was widespread enthusiasm, one night, when the report came in that a large Confederate force, supposed to be Fitzhugh Lee's, was in movement somewhere on our left. In the second report, which immediately telescoped the first, this large force dwindled down to a small squad thrown forward—from an Alabama regiment, as we found out later—to establish an advanced picket line. A portion of Company A was selected to look into the move, and dislodge or capture the post. I got leave to accompany Lieutenant Kane and the thirty-five men detailed for duty.

"We started from camp at about four o'clock of an ugly April morning, with just enough light in the sky to make a ghastly outline of everything, and a wind from the foothills that pricked like needles. Insignificant and scarcely noticed details, when they chance to precede some startling event, have an odd fashion of storing themselves away in one's memory. It all seems like something that happened yesterday, that tramp through a landscape that would have done credit to a nightmare—the smell of the earth thick with strange flowering shrubs; the over-leaning branches that dashed handfuls of wet into our faces; the squirrel that barked at us from a persimmon tree, and how Private Duffy raised a laugh by singing out, 'Shut up, ye young Rebil!" and brought down upon himself a curt reprimand from Kane; for we were then beyond our own lines, and silence was wholesome. The gayety gradually died out of us as we advanced into the *terra incognita* of the enemy, and we became a file of phantoms stealing through the gloaming.

"Owing to a stretch of swamp and a small stream that tried to head us off in a valley, it was close upon sunrise when we reached the point aimed at. The dawn was already getting in its purple work behind the mountain ranges; very soon the daylight would betray us—and we had planned to take the picket by surprise. For five or ten minutes the plan seemed a dead failure; but presently we saw that we had them. Our approach had evidently not been discovered. The advantages were still in our favor, in spite of the daybreak having overtaken us.

"A coil of wet-wood smoke rising above the treetops, where it was blown into threads by the wind, showed us our nearness to the enemy. Their exact position was ascertained by one of our scouts who crawled through the underbrush and got within a hundred feet of the unsuspecting bivouac.

"On the flattened crest of a little knoll, shut in by dwarf cedars and with a sharp declivity on the side opposite us, an infantry officer and twelve or fifteen men were preparing to breakfast. In front of a hut built of boughs and at some distance from the spot where the rifles were stacked, a group in half undress was sniffing the morning air. A sentinel, with his gun leaning against a stump, was drinking something out of a gourd as unconcernedly as thank you. Such lack of discipline and utter disregard of possible danger were common enough in both armies in the early days of the war. 'The idea of burning green wood on a warpath!' growled the scout. 'If them tenderfoots was in the Indian country their scalps wouldn't be on their empty heads a quarter of an hour.'

"We didn't waste a moment preparing to rush the little

post. A whispered order was passed along not to fire before we sprang from cover, and then the word would be given. There was a deathly stillness, except that the birds began to set up a clatter, as they always do at dawn. I remember one shrill little cuss that seemed for all the world to be trying to sound a note of alarm. We scarcely dared draw breath as we moved stealthily forward and up the incline. The attacking party, on the right, was led by Kane and comprised about two-thirds of the detachment; the remainder was to be held in reserve under me. The row of cedars hung with creeper hid us until we were within forty or fifty yards of the encampment, and then the assaulting column charged.

"What happened then—I mean the dark and fatal thing that happened—I didn't witness; but twenty pairs of eyes witnessed it, and a score of tongues afterward bore testimony. I did not see Lieutenant Kane until the affair was over.

"Though the Confederates were taken wholly unawares, the first shot was fired by them, for just as our men came into the open the sentinel chanced to pick up his musket. A scattering volley followed from our side, and a dozen gray figures, seen for a moment scuttling here and there, seemed to melt into the smoke which had instantly blotted out nearly everything. When the air cleared a little, Kane's men were standing around in disorder on the deserted plateau. A stack of arms lay sprawling on the ground and an iron kettle of soup or coffee, suspended from a wooden tripod, was simmering over the blaze of newly lighted fagots. How in the devil, I wondered, had the picket guard managed to slip through their hands? What had gone wrong?

"It was only on the return march that I was told, in

broken words, what had taken place. Lieutenant Kane had botched the business—he had shown the white feather! The incredible story took only a few words in the telling.

"Kane had led the charge with seeming dash and valor, far in advance of the boys, but when the Confederate officer, who was pluckily covering the flight of the picket, suddenly wheeled and with sweeping sabre rushed toward Kane, the West Pointer broke his stride, faltered, and squarely fell back upon the line hurrying up the slope to his support. The action was so unexpected and amazing that the men came to a dead halt, as if they had been paralyzed in their tracks, and two priceless minutes were lost. When the ranks recovered from their stupor, not a gray blouse was anywhere to be seen, save that of the sentry lying dead at the foot of the oak stump.

"That was the substance of the hurried account given me by Sergeant Berwick. It explained a thing which had puzzled me not a little. When I reached the plateau myself, immediately after the occurrence of the incident, Kane's men were standing there indecisive, each staring into his comrade's face in a dazed manner. Then their eyes had turned with one accord upon Lieutenant Kane. That combined glance was as swift, precise, and relentless as a volley from a platoon. Kane stood confronting them, erect, a trifle flushed, but perfectly cool, with the point of his sabre resting on the toe of one boot. He couldn't have appeared cooler on a dress parade. Something odd and dramatic in the whole situation set me wondering. The actors in the scene preserved their hesitating attitude for only twenty seconds or so, and then the living picture vanished in a flash, like a picture thrown from the kinetoscope, and was replaced by another. Kane stepped forward two paces, and as his sword cut a swift half circle in the air, the command rang out in the old resonant, bell-like tones, 'Fall in, men!' I shall never forget how he looked every inch the soldier at that moment. But they—they knew!

"There was no thought of pursuing the escaped picket with the chances of bringing up against an entire regiment, probably somewhere in the neighborhood. The men silently formed into line, a guard was detailed to protect the rear of the column, and we began our homeward march.

"That march back to Camp Blenker was a solemn busi-, ness. Excepting for the fact that we were on the double-quick and the drum taps were lacking, it might have been a burial. Not a loud word was spoken in the ranks, but there was a deal of vigorous thinking. I noticed that Second Lieutenant Rollins and three or four others never took their eyes off of Jefferson Kane. If he had made a motion to get away, I rather fancy it would have gone hard with him.

"We got into camp on schedule time, and in less than fifteen minutes afterward Jefferson Kane's name was burning on every lip. Marconi's wireless telegraph was anticipated that afternoon in Camp Blenker. On a hundred intersecting currents of air the story of the lieutenant's disgrace sped from tent to tent throughout the brigade.

"At first nobody would believe it—it was some sell the boys had put up. Then the truth began to gain ground; incredulous faces grew serious; it was a grim matter. The shadow of it gathered and hung over the whole encampment. A heavy gloom settled down upon the members of Company A, for the stigma was especially theirs. There were a few who would not admit that their lieutenant had been guilty of cowardice, and loyally held out to the end. While conceding the surface facts in the case, they contended that the lieutenant had a sudden faint, or an attack of momentary delirium. Similar instances were recalled. They had happened time and again. Anybody who doubted the boy's pluck was an idiot. A braver fellow than Jeff Kane never buckled a sword belt. That vertigo idea, however, didn't cut much ice, as you youngsters of today would phrase it. There were men who did not hesitate to accuse Lieutenant Kane of intending to betray the detachment into the hands of the Confederates. Possibly he didn't start out with that purpose, it might have occurred to him on the spot; the opportunity had suggested it; if there had been more than a picket guard on hand he would have succeeded. But the dominant opinion was summed up by Corporal Simms. 'He just showed the white feather, and that's all there is about it. He didn't mean nothin', he was just scared silly.'

"In the meantime Kane had shut himself in his tent on the slant of a hill, and was not seen again, excepting for half a moment when he flung back the flap and looked down upon the parade ground with its radiating white-walled streets. What report he had made of the expedition, if he had made any report, did not transpire. Within an hour after our return to camp a significant meeting of the captains of the regiment had been convened at headquarters. Of course a court-martial was inevitable. Though Lieutenant Kane had not as yet been placed under actual arrest, he was known to be under surveillance. At noon that day, just as the bugle was sounding, Jefferson Kane shot himself."

The Major made an abrupt gesture with his one hand, as if to brush away the shadow of the tragedy.

"That was over forty years ago," he continued, meditatively, "but the problem discussed then has been discussed
at odd intervals ever since. In a sort of spectral way, the
dispute has outlasted nine-tenths of those who survived
the war. Differences of opinion hang on like old pensioners
or the rheumatism. Whenever four or five graybeards of
our regiment get together, boring one another with 'Don't
you remember,' the subject is pretty sure to crop up.
Some regard Kane's suicide as a confession of guilt,
others as corroborative proof of the mental derangement
which first showed itself in his otherwise inexplicable de-
failance before a mere handful of the enemy—a West
Pointer! So we have it, hot and heavy, over a man who
nearly half a century ago ceased to be of any importance."

"What is your own diagnosis of the case, Major?" asked
young Dr. Atwood, who always carried the shop about
with him.

"Personally," returned the Major, "I acquit Kane of dis-
loyalty, and I don't believe that he was exactly a coward.
He hadn't the temperament. I will confess that I'm a little
mixed. Sometimes I imagine that that first glimpse of his
own people somehow rattled him for an instant, and the
thing was done. But whether that man was a coward or a
traitor, or neither, is a question which has never definitely
been settled."

"Major," I said, hesitating a little, "I think I can, in a
way, settle it—or, at least, throw some light upon it."

"You?" The Major, with a half-amused air, looked up at
me from under his shaggy, overhanging eyebrows. "Why,
you were not born when all this happened."

"No, I was not born then. My knowledge in the matter
is something very recent. While wintering in the South, two
or three years ago, I became acquainted, rather intimately

acquainted, with the family of Jefferson Kane—that is, with his brother and sister."

"So?"

"It was not until after the surrender of Lee that Jefferson's death was known as a certainty to his family—the manner of it is probably not known to them at this hour. Indeed, I am positive of it. They have always supposed that he died on the field or in the hospital."

"The records at the War Department could have enlightened them," said the Major.

"They did not care to inquire. He had passed out of their lives; his defection never was forgiven. The Confederate officer before whose sword Lieutenant Kane recoiled that day was his father."

"So!"

"Captain Peyton Kane was a broken man after that meeting. He never spoke of it to a living soul, save one— his wife, and to her but once. Captain Kane was killed in the second day's battle at Gettysburg."

My words were followed by a long silence. The room was so still that we could hear the soft pelting of the snow against the windowpanes.

Then the old Major slowly rose from his chair and took up the empty glass beside him, not noticing that it was empty until he lifted it part way to his lips. "Boys," he said, very gently, "only blank cartridges are fired over soldiers' graves. Here's to their memory—the father and the son!"

Other stories, mirthful and serious, were told later on; but the Major did not speak again. He sat there in the dying glow of the firelight, inattentive, seemingly remote in an atmosphere of his own, brooding, doubtless, on

"Old, unhappy, far-off things,
And battles long ago."

The Banjo String

BY LOUIS REED

"Yessuh," said Captain Bob Pennybacker, "at the time this little skirmish was fought, it rated more newspaper space than Gettysburg. Believe it or not, right here was the end of the most darin' invasion ever attempted in North America."

Captain Bob and I had known each other scarcely five minutes. From different directions we had come to Portland, Ohio, to look at the new monument commemorating the Battle of Buffington's Island, and had begun to talk, as strangers will at such times, about the battle. The captain was a very aged man—past ninety—but he was a spry, hearty old fellow, and had made a long automobile trip to get there. When he mentioned that he believed himself

to be the only surviving member of Morgan's Raiders, and
perhaps the only man still living who had taken part in
the Battle of Buffington's Island, I gave him my undivided
journalistic attention.

"This is news," thought I to myself. "Why, it's nearly
seventy years since this battle was fought—the whole allotted span of life. What a yarn this would be for Harry
Gill and the *News!*"

"Yessuh," the captain went on, "the place looks about
like it did then, except for the lock and the dam. It ain't
changed much that I can see. It was early mornin', you
know. He was asleep over there by the schoolhouse. Judah
came up that road, and Hobson this. There was a whoop
and a volley. We knowed then the hell had busted for
sure, and started to run. And just then, when I needed it
the most, I found that the banjo string was gone."

"That," I remarked, "sounds like a story."

"Does it?" the captain replied. "Well, I won't be surprised if it is. I ain't got nothin' to do till the boy gets
back. You ain't neither? All right; listen."

In the spring of '63 (said Captain Bob), the armies in
Tennessee set there on the Duck River for months and
months just lookin' at each other. It got so the front-line
pickets would stop on their rounds and talk to each other.
You'd likely hear a Confederate holler across the river and
say, "Well, Yank, how's the rats over there? Are they nice
and fat like they ought to be?" And the Yank maybe
would reply, "They ain't done so well lately, Reb, but
from all I can hear, business is apt to pick up in a year
or two." Then they'd both laugh, and go on about their
business. It begun to look like the war would end in a general handshakin'.

I was only twenty-one then, but I had the bars of a captain on my shoulder straps—a captain in a brigade that before we set down to play tiddlywinks on the Duck River was noted for bein' the hardest-ridin', most hell-for-leather cavalry outfit in the world. And that ain't rhetoric, mistuh. The men you hear about these days are Lee and Grant, and Johnson and Sherman and suchlike, but in 1863 the one Southern general that sent chills up and down the spines of every blasted Yankee from here to Portland, Maine, was nobody but Morgan. Ask the old-timers. When Lee invaded Pennsylvania that was a matter of military strategy, but when Morgan crossed the Ohio it was God save our souls and the Devil take the hindmost. Yessuh.

Morgan was in his thirty-eighth year then. I can see him yet, spick-and-span in his new gray uniform, with his long hair hangin' over his shoulders and a little feather stuck in his cavalry hat. Most people think of Morgan as he was on his raids, when dirt and dust and sweat was part of the day's work, but behind the lines he was your finest example of the dashin' stage soldier. He even used perfume on his hair, and the women he had—well, the less said of Morgan's women, the better.

Morgan was a man that could make fun of you to your face and make you like it. I remember when he promoted me to captain—a striplin' of twenty I was then—he said: "Pennybacker, from now on you're captain of Troop C. Don't fall off a horse and break your neck this summer, Captain. If things keep on this way, I may have to make you a general."

That was Morgan for you! Rough, and sharp tongued as an old woman. Yet his men knowed his bark was worse than his bite. They'd follow him to hell and back again, and I guess some of 'em did.

All those months while we set there twiddlin' our thumbs on the Duck River, Morgan was tryin' to put over a project with the commandin' general. That was Bragg. It was noised around that Lee was gettin' ready to invade Pennsylvania. Everybody knowed that. The Yanks knowed it; every farmer, housewife, and private soldier in the South knowed it. What Morgan wanted was an army of his own.

"Give me ten thousand horses and men," he told Bragg, "and I'll cut a swath from here to Harrisburg, right through Kentucky, Indiana, and Ohio."

To understand what that meant you got to know your geography. From the Duck River to Louisville on the Ohio was three hundred miles. From Louisville to Harrisburg over the windin' roads was at least twelve hundred more. All Morgan asked was to advance fifteen hundred miles through the enemy's territory. He was goin' to do it, you understand, in spite of the Union Army in Tennessee and Kentucky, the organized militia of four states, his own ignorance of the country, and all the gunboats in the Ohio Valley!

Bragg said he was crazy, and I don't know but what he was. Bragg wouldn't give him the horses or the men he asked for. Instead, Bragg said, "General, here's your old brigade of two thousand men. We don't want Judah's cavalry around here when the big push starts, so run up to Louisville, like a good boy, and get him out of the way. And remember, General, whatever you do, don't stick your head out of Kentucky."

So that was that.

Morgan kept his mouth shut for the time bein', though his actions showed the rest of us plain enough what he thought of Bragg. After that order came through to strike north for Louisville, I know for a fact that he never slept night or day for a week. He sent out orders so fast that forty brigades couldn't keep up with 'em. We had to polish all the equipment, and shoe the horses, and clean the guns; and when that was finished, we had to do it all over again. When he wasn't prowlin' around at night, tryin' to catch somebody off guard, he'd amuse himself firin' off pistols in his tent. Yessuh. You could hear him all night long firin' his pistols, and when you went there you never knowed but what he'd stick a bullet in you. At other times he wouldn't say a word to nobody, just sit silent for hours outside his tent, starin' off at the sky line. Then, finally, when every horse was properly shod, and every piece of equipment shinin' like an Indian, and every soldier on the place rarin' to go, it was the first of July and Morgan said this is the night we dash north to Louisville.

I often think afterward, though it don't mean much at the time, how queer it was that the very day we're to leave I got a letter from my mammy over in the hills of North Carolina. It was a short letter, wrote in pencil on a piece of packin' paper, and it read, "Bob, your grandpappy has broke the A string on his banjo. He can't find none at the stores here. You know how Grandpappy likes to play the banjo, so the first chance you get, send him a string. Be sure it's an A string, for that's the one that's broke."

Now you may think a little thing like that don't amount to much in the face of a campaign, but that's when little things often mean the most. I was a poor boy when I joined the army as a private. I'd been away two years without seein' my folks. That banjo string made me homesick. It brought back memories of the hill farm where I spent my boyhood, of the cabin with the honeysuckle in the yard, of such things as new hay and fresh eggs and creamy milk, and most of all, of Grandpappy sittin' in front of the fire with his banjo. All my life I'd listened to that banjo. It had a place in my life I can't hardly explain, for music, you know, is like God and religion, and life and death. It's the thing that makes the day's work a little less hard, the year's sufferin' a little less painful, God Himself a little less remote.

Here, have a cigar.

That afternoon I went up and down the line of tents one way, and sent my orderly, Tom Barnes, the other, huntin' for that string. We tried every commissary and canteen in the district, and every banjo player we could hear of, but we couldn't find an A string that was loose nowheres. So, towards night, the last thing before we struck out on the long trail to Louisville, I set down and wrote my mammy that I couldn't send the string then, but I would as soon as I got one.

You been a soldier yourself? In the last war? I thought so. Well, styles of fightin' change. I don't know how it is with you, but I always think they took the fun out of soldierin' when they broke up the cavalry. I remember that last night on the Duck River like it was yesterday. I can see the long ranks drawn up in formation—the horses sniffin' excitement and prancin' in the lines, the men stiff and tense in their saddles. And out in front was Morgan, ridin' up and down, up and down, with the feather in his hat showin' against the sky.

Then, all of a sudden, the ranks broke and wheeled. We was off with no other sound at first than the patter of the horseshoes on the dirt road. The word came down the line to "cross the river at Ford Nineteen, and then ride like hell for Kentucky"—and that's what we done.

The Duck River is in rollin' country, and the Yankees had outposts on all the hills. We could hear 'em as we splashed through the river, shoutin' the warnin' from hill to hill that Rebs was breakin' through; and a little later we heard the splash of Judah's cavalry beneath us. The next mornin' in Kentucky, there he was at Marrowbone ready to greet us.

That brush with Judah's men at Marrowbone, I may say, went off exactly like Morgan figured it would. The poor Yankee horsemen, you see, had been up all night, and had to rest. So Morgan called in all his commissioned officers, and said, "You see them Yankee bluecoats in the road yonder? Well, I call you in here for a purpose. I want to see what county they'll be in two hours from now."

As it turned out, they was in the next county. We followed 'em till we got tired and quit. Then we stripped such prisoners as we had of their shirts and shoes, shootin' a few for good measure, took the horses we needed in place of them that was killed, and called the roll for the next dash to the Green River.

After this little skirmish at Marrowbone we was still close to the Duck River and the army in Tennessee, so Morgan halted to send back dispatches. That's when I found the banjo string. I don't know what to say about that except it was unexpected and unusual, and yet the most natural thing in the world. Yessuh, in spite of everything, it was perfectly natural. It come about this way.

The place where we stopped to rest and write the dispatches was a little valley with a patch of woods on one side of the road. Tom Barnes—that's my orderly—and me lay down at the foot of a tree to catch a few winks, for we'd been in the saddle all night and day. But I never got to sleep. There'd been fightin' along that road a little while before. I could hear somebody cryin' back there in the woods. He'd cry awhile, then he'd groan, and then he'd pray.

There wasn't nothin' specially remarkable in that—not
in 1863—but somethin' in his voice sounded familiar. It
wasn't so much what he said as the way he said it. I got to
listenin', and pretty soon it come to me what it was. I said
to myself, "That ain't a white man. He's colored, and if
I'm any judge of voices, he's got North Carolina wrote all
over him."

When I went back there and found him, he was black as
the ace of spades. I said to him, "What's the matter?" And
he said, "I'se knifed, massa, an' de Lawd's a-comin' for
me."

One look showed he was right about that. He had a
bayonet stickin' right through his middle. I asked how it
happened, but he never answered. He quit prayin', and
groanin', and cryin', and just looked at me with pain in his
eyes, like a dumb animal. He grabbed my hand and hung
on to it, like people will when they're dyin', and I sat there
maybe fifteen minutes—maybe half an hour—without
sayin' a word till he died.

Now, suh, it's funny about that man. There I was in enemy
country, with white men dyin' all around me, and liable to
be killed any minute myself. But somehow or other he was
on my mind. I remember I thought to myself, "Maybe he
belongs to somebody that don't know what's happened to
him. Maybe he'll lie out here in these woods and rot before
anybody finds him. Maybe I ought to take him down to the
road, so he'll have an even chance of bein' buried."

I mention these things to show you how natural it was.
He had on blue cotton overalls and a jacket, and I thought
maybe he'd have somethin' on him to show who he was. I
went through his pockets, and found three copper cents
and some sixpenny nails. No papers, nothin' at all to
identify him. Then I noticed I'd missed the watch pocket

of his overalls. That's a crooked pocket. I stuck in my fore-finger like a hook—and pulled out a brand-new A string for a banjo.

I thought afterward there was somethin' more than coincidence back of that, but not then. All I thought then was how lucky it was for Grandpappy. It couldn't have worked out better if I'd planned it all from the beginnin'. So I dragged the man by his feet down to the roadway, put the banjo string in an envelope addressed to my mammy, and handed it to Morgan's dispatch rider, to mail in Ten-nessee. Five minutes later the rider was headed south, while the rest of us was ridin' hell-bent for the Green River.

Somehow when I think of the Green River and Kentucky, the most of what I think of is Morgan. There was so few of us, you see, that pretty near all the time on the road and in the rest camps he was in sight and hearin'. I remember that after the long rest on the Duck River Morgan was bubblin' over with energy and the joy of livin'. He had a mockin' light in his eyes and pride in his smile. You would see him at the head of his column, with his cavalry cloak flyin' in the wind and his big gray hat cocked on the side of his head, and somehow you felt that here was a man worth followin' and fightin' for.

He made you feel that you didn't need the things that other armies carried with 'em. You didn't need doctors and hospitals and nurses, because Morgan's men rode their horses as long as they could, and when they couldn't they rolled off and died. You didn't need rations, or horse feed, or reinforcements, or even siege guns, for four little cannon carried on horseback was all our artillery for the capture of Louisville.

Impossible, you say? Listen, mistuh, you forget Morgan. In them days the very name of Morgan was worth half an army. It was a name spoken of along with Hell, and the Devil and his angels, for Morgan was like the Scourge of God, the one that they said where his horse trod the grass never grew. Yes, suh. If Morgan had wanted to, Louisville would've come down.

We fought five battles in eight days, and at Tebb's Bridge alone we lost ninety men killed. We outrun Judah's three cavalry brigades for three hundred miles. We thrashed the militia right and left, burned ammunition and supply trains, impressed enlistments and shot them that wouldn't, took what we wanted wherever we found it, and in general put the fear of God and the Southern republic into the people of Kentucky.

It took iron men to stand it. Day after day and night after night we spent fourteen, sixteen, eighteen hours in the saddle. We slept, when we did sleep, with our heads pillowed on our horses' sides, and woke with our knives clutched in one hand and our muskets in the other.

It was late at night when we got close to Louisville. We slept in some woods. The next mornin' we could see what was happenin' in the city. The militia and the Home Guards was mountin' the fortifications, but the river in back was filled with ferryboats transportin' the citizens to the other side. It was plain they was plumb scared to death. There was gunboats steamin' up the river and down, and every now and then they'd fire a broadside just to show us they was warlike.

Morgan laughed at that till he almost fell off his horse. He said, "Do you know how many men can take that place? Ten men and a boy. I guess I'll send a company over to try it."

We thought that was a bluff, and it was, but we didn't know then why he was bluffin'. He didn't send ten men and a boy, though. He sent a hundred and thirty, and they had orders just to scare the garrison. Then, with the rest of us, he tore down the river to Brandenburg, where two steamboats manned by Confederate soldiers was tied up at the dock.

We seen Morgan fling himself off his horse, and walk along the bank. He was all smiles as he studied the Indiana shore through his field glasses. Then he came back to one of his colonels and said, "There ain't nothin' but a handful of militia over there, Duke. Start 'em over."

Somebody said, "What're you goin' to do, General? Take Cincinnati?" And Morgan said, "Hell, no. I ain't goin' to take Cincinnati. I'm goin' to take Harrisburg."

Yessuh, that's what he said. With one little brigade he was goin' to march twelve hundred miles through the enemy's country to Harrisburg. You say you know he was crazy? You're right, but if you remember your geography, this little monument is nine hundred miles from the Duck River in Tennessee. He belonged to that crazy breed of Pizarro, and Cortez, and William Walker, and maybe Alexander and Napoleon. He had dreams of conquest, and when he started to ferry his troops to Indiana he looked it.

Now, suh, right then was when I seen the dispatch rider. I mean the one I give the banjo string to at Marrowbone. He oughtn't to be in Bradenburg at all, so far as I could see, so I walked up to him and said, "Well, brothah, how about the banjo string? Did you mail it?"

He said, "No, I didn't have no luck. I never got there. The Yanks almost picked me up outside of Marrowbone, but I caught up with the Brigade at Tebb's Bridge. Here's your letter."

I put the letter in my left breast pocket. We was busy

just then because some Indiana militia on the other side had set up a cannon and was beginnin' to fire both the cannon and muskets across the river. To deal with their cannon Morgan was layin' out his four pieces of artillery. I started to move in Morgan's direction just as Tom Barnes, my orderly, come up beside me. And just then I felt somethin' snap in the front of my blouse and a sharp little stab of pain in my left side.

I said, "Tom, I guess I picked up a Minié ball." Tom reached inside my shirt to locate the blood, but he didn't find none. Nothin' there but a red spot that was goin' to be blue over the heart. He felt of the breast pocket and pulled out the banjo string. The string had been shot in two.

"Too bad," I said. "Grandpappy's lost a banjo string."

I started to toss it away, but Tom caught my arm. "Don't do that," he said. "That string's still long enough for a banjo. Just one end was shot off. Anyhow, it's your luck string. It saved your life. Keep it."

So I kept it. I put it back in my breast pocket and left it there till we got here to Buffington's Island. I got so I believed it was a luck piece too, and I do yet. All the way across Indiana and Ohio, when misfortune followed misfortune, I kept that banjo string next to my heart, and as long as I kept it there, there was hope.

That was an excitin' day at Brandenburg. Morgan silenced the Indiana cannon the first round. Then he sent over two steamboat loads of men without their horses, and what they done to the remainin' militiamen was a plenty. To serve as a warning in the future, they strung some of 'em on grapevines, and draped them from convenient trees near the highway. Afterwards we all had a set-to with a Federal gunboat, but late that afternoon our little army—

swelled to about twenty-five hundred men by Kentucky enlistments—was in Indiana.

Well, suh, I don't know what kind of a country Indiana is now, but in '63 it was fine. Maybe you know how it was in the South then—the fields lyin' idle, the stores empty, the spirit of the people beginnin' to break. But Indiana was different. Why, you'd never know they was havin' a war in Indiana. The fields was ploughed and tended, the barns loaded with hay and grain, the whole country filled with peace and plenty. We got things to eat in Indiana that we hadn't tasted for months, like fried chicken and blackberry pie, and the stores was full of things you couldn't buy in the South for love or money.

Morgan got rich in Indiana. That's a thing most people don't know about. The very day we crossed the river he said to me, "I got news that the banks along the river are sendin' deposits to Chicago by messenger. It seems like they wasn't expectin' us, and the trains are tied up. Now here's a guide to take you up above Salem tonight—you and your men. Stop everybody that comes along, and look at their saddlebags. But don't take nothin' but money. Understand?"

I said, "Yessuh," and went to work. I remember I kept thinkin' of my luck piece that night, and, whether it helped or not, we made a real haul. We got over $90,000 in gold, currency, and greenbacks. I never knowed there was so much money in the world. I turned it all over to Morgan, and he said, "Pennybacker, I'll remember you. One of these days I'll make you a general."

That's the way he was in them days—tall, straight, proud, and dignified. It seemed like he growed up a little in Indiana. There was still the same eager look in his eyes and the same mockin' smile on his lips, but he seemed older, like a man with heavy responsibilities. From the day we crossed the Ohio he was Kingfish of the countryside and master of Indiana.

Yessuh, them first days in Indiana was fine. We had fine things to eat, and all kinds of goods out of the stores we looted, and it seemed like the Indiana women was right glad to have us, for they baked cakes and pies, and put 'em out where we could find 'em. There wasn't even no bushwhackers around, for all the men had gone north to join the militia.

Maybe we'd a stayed in Indiana for some time gettin' fat and lazy if it wasn't for that newspaper Morgan picked up in Corydon. It don't hardly seem possible now, but this was a week after Gettysburg, and none of us knowed it. We'd been cut off that long from the rest of the army. That newspaper showed that these rumors about Lee in Pennsylvania was right. It made him mad as a wet hen.

"Do you know what that jackass Lee has gone and done?" he said. "The old fool is givin' up the campaign. That's what he's doin'. He's fallin' back to Virginia."

Now, suh, that was sure bad news for us. If Lee got back to Virginia before we got to Pennsylvania, we'd have to fight through the whole Yankee army of the Potomac to reach him. He was still over a thousand miles from Harrisburg, and the people of Indiana wasn't joinin' up with us like we thought they would. As a matter of fact, we learned from that same paper that the Governor of Indiana was sendin' sixty thousand more men against us.

You'll say that the sensible thing then was to pull up stakes and get back to Kentucky while the gettin' was good. There ain't no doubt about that, but if you notice it, this campaign wasn't based much on sober judgment. It was one of them unsensible things that almost succeeded anyhow, and when they do, they are miracles.

Takin' to cover wasn't the kind of fightin' Morgan was used to. He said, "Men, we got to get to Pennsylvania and pull that old blockhead out of a hole. He ought to see then what an army can do when it gets the lead out of its tail."

So, instead of hustlin' back to Brandenburg and makin' tracks for the Duck River in Tennessee, we hoisted the war flag and marched eastward.

You wasn't in the cavalry, of course. You don't know what it means to sit on a horse twenty-two hours out of twenty-four. What it takes to face a hundred thousand militiamen, three brigades of Federal cavalry—Judah again—and so many bushwhackers that God Himself couldn't stop to count them. Them was the days when we done what we didn't think human bein's could, for we slept on our horses six nights in succession. Compared to Ohio, Kentucky was baby play. We used up our last ounce of energy, and wore ourselves down to skin and bones. But it was Ohio that finally broke us.

Give me a match.

One thing about Ohio that we couldn't believe was the number of able-bodied men that joined the militia. The South had already called up its reserves, and, till we run into these new armies, we supposed it was the same way in the North. But the Governor of Ohio raised fifty-five thousand new volunteers in one day. They gathered at Hamilton while we was still in Indiana, and sent Morgan word not to cross the state line.

You know what Morgan done about that? The first thing he done was to burn all the bridges behind him so he couldn't retreat, and he moved on Hamilton. He gathered up all the horses in the district, shot the livestock, burned the crops, and then, when the militia was ready to crush him, he run off and left 'em. He struck south to Cincinnati so fast that people actually drowned themselves in the river tryin' to swim to Kentucky. He passed through the outskirts of Cincinnati, looted some stores, blew up some more bridges, and dashed north and east on the highway to Columbus. From then on it was less a campaign than a foot race. Morgan was on his way to Pennsylvania.

He was at Piketon, Ohio, when the news come that Lee had retreated out of Pennsylvania. That was a real piece of hard luck. We'd come so far then it was too late to turn back, and with Lee out of Pennsylvania, it was useless to go on. I wish you could've heard Morgan swear at Lee. He said, among other things, that Lee as a general would make a good horse doctor, and that he really had less sense than that other half-wit, Jefferson Davis.

He took out his maps. "What we have to do," he said, "is get out of Ohio in a hurry. There's too many soldiers here, and too many bushwhackers. If Lee'd done what he ought to, it wouldn't be so bad, but now we got to fight all the bloomin' Yankees in the North. Here's a ford across the Ohio at Buffington's Island. West Virginia's mountain country. If we cross there, we can keep to the hills and catch up with Lee in the Valley of Virginia."

It was still five hundred miles across the Allegheny Mountains to the Valley of Virginia, but when you come right down to it, there wasn't much else he could do. He'd disobeyed Bragg's orders, and couldn't go back to Tennessee nohow; and it wasn't no use goin' on to Pennsylvania; and with the cavalry and militia pressin' him from behind, he couldn't sit down and wait. So he put away his maps and set the course to Buffington's Island.

It was after we left Piketon that I come to have faith in the A string, and believe me, faith in somethin' was necessary. It started to rain. Not occasional summer showers, mind you, but a steady drizzlin' downpour that lasted for days and bogged the roads with mud. Besides the weather, we had to contend with a plague of the orn'riest bushwhackers we ever run into. They was worse than forty armies. Always poppin' away at us from the underbrush, every day cuttin' us down little by little. Firin' back at 'em wasted our ammunition, so that when we got here to Buffington's Island, in addition to everything else, we was short of cartridges.

But all the way across Ohio I wore that banjo string over my heart, and I never got a scratch. No, suh, not even a close call. I seen men shot down all around me. I seen 'em fall off their horses from exhaustion and get themselves crushed by the hoofs of other horses behind 'em, but I done my twenty-two hours a day in safety, and got here feelin' as well as a man could expect to under the circumstances.

We stopped to rest, as I say, over by that schoolhouse. The river was flooded and it was late, but we figured Judah and the cavalry was a hundred miles back. We didn't know about him helpin' himself upriver with the gunboats. I remember Tom Barnes and me lay down side by side. I took off my shoes—the first time in ten days—and Tom took off his shoes. We placed 'em on the ground beside us. I was already half asleep, I guess, for I remember takin' the banjo string out of my pocket, lookin' at it, and then droppin' it in one of the shoes.

The next thing I knowed it was daylight. We'd slept there in the mud all night. I was cold and cramped, but for a while I didn't move at all. I just lay there on my back lookin' off to the east where the fog was raisin'. I seen some of the other soldiers beginnin' to stir, and rolled over to wake Tom. That's when it happened.

There wasn't a guard on duty nowheres. They was all sound asleep. Judah's men had come up to the shelter of that knoll there durin' the night. Hobson, with a detachment we didn't know about before, come to about here. While I lay there lookin' at the sky they was crouched ready to charge. When they come it was yellin' and shootin', and there we was stretched out on our backs, and part of us not even dressed.

You see what the monument says—seven hundred Confederate prisoners. That tells part of the story. The rest of it is about them that got away. There was about a thousand of us, I guess, that put on our clothes as we ran, and took to flight in our shirttails. I remember stickin' my feet in my shoes and jumpin' on the horse without tightenin' the saddle girth. The saddle slipped, and I come down on my head. I thought, "Where's the A string?" It wasn't in my shoes. Not havin' time to hunt for it then, I yanked up the girth and started up the valley without it. The first thing I knowed, there we was—what was left of us—ridin' hell-bent for Long Bottom with Morgan himself leadin' the pack.

We stopped at Long Bottom, because the Yankees was busy herdin' the prisoners here. The river there was brown and muddy, and runnin' saw logs at the flood crest. Morgan took one look at it and said, "Men, flood or no flood, we got to swim it." And he proceeded then and there to do it. He divided the survivors into four companies, and led the first company into the water himself. I was in that company too, and I remember the feather on Morgan's hat was a little drooped as he rode his horse into the river.

My horse got scared and throwed me out of the saddle.

When I finally got him quieted, I seen a picture of the river ahead that's stayed with me all these years. It was a picture of swirlin' brown waters carryin' brush and saw logs, of white foam and bubbles and eddies, and whirlpools. And straight out ahead of me was a line of black dots on the surface of the water—always two dots together—that was the heads of horses and men.

You've seen the Ohio at flood time when the river rages and swells and a man on its surface looks as puny and helpless as a skipper bug. What I wonder most about now is how any of us ever got through. I remember watchin' the dots ahead as they neared the swell of the brush and the saw logs. I seen two big logs push a man off his horse, and I had a glimpse of the man's white face turned up to heaven before he sunk out of sight. Then I was there in the midst of it myself, fightin' for life in a whirlpool of white foam and crashin' timbers weighin' hundreds of tons.

I thought to myself, "I lost the A string, and I'll never make it," but I kept tryin' just the same. That's when I first realized the value of brains in a battle against the forces of nature. The big logs was destructive, but they was blind, and the river that carried 'em was blind too. I could meet 'em in a certain way, and push 'em off me with my hand. They was dangerous only when they come in pairs, or in threes or fours, and I found I could miss those by divin'. I made the horse dive too, but that drowned him. I felt the bridle pullin' me down, and let him go. When I come up there was another horse without a rider splashin' at my side, and I took charge of him.

I suppose it wasn't really so long, but it seemed like I was there for hours. I remember all of a sudden I come out of the brush and the logs to a place where the water was calmer. There was still a line of dots ahead of me, but fewer than before. In the distance I could see a green shore line that I knowed was West Virginia. And just then a face come out of the water at my side, a face that was death white under the mud streaks. I looked at it and stretched out my hand. It was the face of my orderly, Tom Barnes.

I grabbed him by the hair, and hung on to the pommel of my saddle with the other hand. I thought he wasn't dead yet; if I got him to shore I might revive him. I kept his head out of the water while the horse pulled us onto the bank. The first man I saw when we got there was Morgan, but his hat with the feather was gone.

Tom was dead. I found that out first thing, and left him. Morgan was walkin' up and down the shore. As I come up to him, I noticed that he looked old and tired. His shoulders was drooped, and the old mockin' smile was gone. There was a cannon shot just then down the river. Morgan stopped to listen. I saw his jaw shoot out with some of his old fire and determination.

He turned to me and said, "Pennybacker, those are gunboats. The others can't make it. You're the rankin' officer here, so take these men and disappear in the hills."

I said, "What're you goin' to do, General? Ain't you comin' with us?"

He said, "No. My men on the other side need me most. I'm goin' back."

Then he held out a hand that was white from exposure in the water, said, "Good luck," and turned to the river to swim back again to Ohio. We had to cheer him, suh. Whatever else you say of Morgan, he was a soldier and a man. Nothin' but death could stop him. We heard later he got across, too—swum the Ohio twice at flood time, and the second time he swam it alone. He went on toward Pennsylvania two hundred miles more till they finally got him, and put him in the penitentiary at Columbus. You know the rest of that. They never built the penitentiary that'd hold Morgan. He escaped back to Tennessee, raised a new brigade, and was finally shot and killed at Greenville in 1864.

We was safer in West Virginia than in Ohio, for the pursuit followed Morgan's main band. I buried poor Tom there on the bank of the river with my own hands. Before I dropped him in his grave I said a little service, and I took off his shoes, because shoes was a thing we didn't bury with no man. It was what I found in one of them shoes that made me cry, suh. Pressed down in the toe of his left shoe—the shoe that was next to mine at Portland the night before—was the A string.

Yessuh. I never got over that. All the way up that valley with the Yankees shootin' up the turf behind us, and across that ragin' river, old Tom carried the A string.

We got away, suh. Averell's men chased us all the way across West Virginia, but we outran 'em. We reached the Kanawha, struck south through the mountains, and then we broke up and went home.

It was a proud day for me, suh, when I rode up the old trail to my mammy's cabin. I was a boy when I went away, but when I come back, I was a man. I could see the hills idle and wasted with the blight of the war, but the sun shone just as bright as it did before, and the birds sung just as sweet. When I got to the last bend in the road, there was the cabin with the honeysuckle around it, and old Grandpappy himself at the gate.

I had the A string in my hand. Grandpappy uncoiled it

without sayin' a word, flicked it with his fingernail, and went back in the house. When my mammy come out to me there was music in the air, for Grandpappy was playin' the old tunes that seemed somehow to wipe out the bitterness.

Cadmus Henry, Balloon Observer

BY WALTER D. EDMONDS

Cadmus picked up the despatch. He could leave it till
Captain Bryan returned; but, on the other hand, as he was
in charge of the office, maybe he ought to open it to see
whether it was important. After a brief hesitation he persuaded himself he ought to open it; but the despatch was
not important. It was no more than a request from General
Johnston to General Magruder for a qualified observer.
The man, General Johnston wrote, would need a thorough
knowledge of the Peninsula and a good comprehension
of the general situation, and he was to report to General
Johnston before nightfall.

Cadmus felt cheated. He had half hoped there might be

an emergency and that he could take some part in it. He
got up drearily to take the message across to the ad-
jutant's desk, but as he laid it down there, his eyes went
over the wording of the message and suddenly his heart
skipped a beat. General Johnston hadn't asked for an
officer; he had merely asked for a qualified observer.

It didn't take Cadmus more than a second to make up
his mind about it; just long enough to step to the back
window. The coast was clear, so he went to find General
Magruder, who was at his own desk in the act of com-
position. The general wrote, Cadmus thought, a little the
way he rode a horse, at full gallop. "Come in, Mr. Henry,"
he said with the faint lisp that came curiously from such an
imposing figure of a man. "Just let me finish this sentence."
It must have been a good one, for it covered more than
nine lines before it hit a period and the general dropped
his pen and reached out his hand with almost a single
motion.

"Let's see what you have, Mr. Henry."

"It has just come in, sir." Cadmus couldn't keep the excitement out of his voice. He could feel the shakes getting
a hold on him, and he froze onto them, like a bird dog
working up to a point. "I thought I'd better bring it in
now."

The general looked up.

"It's not very important, you know, Mr. Henry."

Cadmus had stopped himself shaking, but he was so
stiff that for an instant he didn't think his jaw was going
to open. When it did, his voice came out louder than necessary. "I'd like to volunteer for the job, sir."

There were some people who thought Bankhead
Magruder was a fool and others who considered him
pompous and a show-off, and there were a few who won-

dered if he had ever quite grown up. He said now, with a sober face, "I suppose you've consulted Captain Bryan."

"Captain Bryan was out, sir." Cadmus looked at the handsome, florid face framed in the elaborate whiskers and suddenly he took his courage in both hands. "He'd never allow me to go," he blurted out. "He wants to keep me clerking the way I've been since I got here. I can't fight this war at a desk, sir. I've got to get out of that office. I've just absolutely got to."

He stopped himself short and swallowed hard. He had the dry swallows. He hadn't meant to raise his voice that way, but General Magruder didn't appear to have noticed.

"I know how you feel, Mr. Henry. We all of us get taped down in different ways, but you've had a dose of it. Do you think you're qualified for the work?"

"I know the Peninsula, sir. Before my father died he used to take me round with him on his calls. He was a doctor. He was a good one," Cadmus said with the pride in his voice he had first learned from his mother. "I've seen most of the papers going through the office, too, and I know where our people are, pretty well."

"Well," the general said, "you're very young. But I'll give you a letter to General Johnston. If you can convince him, you can have the detail." He wrote a few rapid lines and handed the sheet to Cadmus. "There you are. I wish you luck, Mr. Henry." He shook hands with Cadmus and said casually, "That's a fine pair of boots you have on. Would you mind letting me have the name of your boot maker?"

Cadmus gave it. His estimation of Great Uncle Eppa's knowledge of the world had been considerably raised. He saluted the general and went out of the room as happy as a fiddlestring. He could even feel a twinge of conscience when Captain Bryan finally returned; he could afford to now, for there was nothing Captain Bryan could do about his leaving.

But the captain made no attempt to stop him. He merely grinned sardonically. "You go right along, Mr. Henry. You go right along. If you're going to become a hero, you might as well become one now as later. I doubt if General Johnston will take you, anyway. You're too young for the work. But if he does, you'll probably get into hot water. Mighty hot," the captain added, rather as if he hoped so.

Cadmus didn't put much dependence in what the captain said. He thought Captain Bryan was just jawing because he was mad. It didn't seem likely that General Johnston would turn him down when he came with General Magruder's personal recommendation.

It wasn't any distance over to Lee's house where General Johnston's headquarters were, but Cadmus got out the brown mare. He took her down toward the river road a piece and let her travel, for she was fresh as paint with all her idle days, and he told her to have her fun—she was going to have work soon enough, he told her.

The sun was setting when he turned back. The color from it came through the trees and picked out threads of light in the water-filled ruts. A section of a battery was having a slow time with the mud, and the men looked up from the two guns and hooted as the mare danced into the ditch to get by. "One of Magruder's little boys," they yelled after him. "Look out you don't spoil them nice new clothes." There was a kind of anger, too, in their voices that made the blood rise uneasily in his face. They looked as if they had been a long time in the rain; their faces had the color of mud, and the teams were irritable and uncertain.

But then he had the road to himself and the twilight started coming into the woods and he realized that he had better get back in a hurry. The mare was willing, for the Union batteries were opening up all along the line and there was a new deep undertone over toward Yorktown, as though some heavy guns had got to work. Now and then, too, there would be outbreaks of musketry that suddenly fused to a single point in the line and then quickly faded out. None of the shells reached in his direction, but it was an unearthly feeling to be alone on a woods road with all that racket going on; and the mare went like a blown leaf.

Cadmus arrived at Lee's house like someone with important news, but the sentry wasn't impressed. He sent in for an officer, and a young lieutenant came out and took Magruder's letter. It was several minutes before he came back for Cadmus and led him inside. They stopped at the door of an inner room, which the lieutenant opened for him.

There were two men in the room and Cadmus didn't have to be told which was Joe Johnston. The other introduced himself as Major Rhett, but Cadmus hardly noticed what he looked like. The general's eyes held him. They were gray and penetrating and they gave nothing away.

"How old are you, Mr. Henry?" he asked, and when Cadmus told him, he said sharply, "He's too young"; and Cadmus didn't like the twist of his thin lips. It looked to him as if Captain Bryan would prove to be right, and a wave of humiliation went through him.

But the major said, "You can hardly blame Mr. Henry for his age."

General Johnston had already picked up some papers.

But he put them down and lifted his head again, and as he studied Cadmus's face, the bitter lines of his mouth softened.

"No," he said. "I don't suppose we can. Sit down, Mr. Henry, while I ask you a few questions."

There were only a few, but it seemed to Cadmus that the general had found out from them most of what there was to know about his life and his experience with the army. He hadn't realized before how little there was to the sum total, and when the general finished, he expected to be told to get out; but instead General Johnston said, "Bring me the big-scale map," and while the major fiddled with some map cases, the general started clearing the papers off a big table at one side of the room.

Cadmus saw that he had probably squeaked by the first part of his examination, and he took heart from it. He made up his mind to do better with the map.

"Take a good look at it, Mr. Henry," the general told him.

It showed the whole end of the Peninsula up nearly to Barhamville. Roads had been marked out, and the better farms, and the defense lines penciled in.

"What are you looking at?" the general asked suddenly.

He was standing next to Cadmus, and he was short enough so Cadmus could look right over his head.

"I was looking at Lee's house; it's marked there," Cadmus said.

"Why?"

"Because that's where I am."

The general was very erect. He had sloping shoulders but he had a wiry quality about him. Once in a while you'll get a little rooster, and he'll dodge and turn and run off and make motions, but when he sets to fight he's wicked as perdition. That was how Joe Johnston looked to Cadmus. In the candlelight his eyes took on some of the hard, clear brightness of a bird's.

He started asking questions about turnpikes and woods, roads and farms and the places where there were fords. Cadmus could tell him almost all those things and even show where the map was wrong. Most Confederate maps of the Peninsula at that time were pretty inaccurate. The Union generals weren't any better off on that score, though, of course, Cadmus couldn't know that.

Then the general made Cadmus go to the far side of the room and asked him a few more questions when he didn't have the map to help him out. But Cadmus was sure of himself now, and he answered as fast as the general asked him, and after only a minute or two the general stopped and rolled up the map and looked across it at Cadmus with an unexpected twinkle in his eyes.

"I wouldn't have thought Bankhead Magruder had it in him."

"Had what in him?" asked the major, who had gone back to some work of his own.

"Sending us the right man. I think Mr. Henry's going to be all right. You'll have to show him the kind of report we need and what sort of information we're after," said the general. "And make out a special order assigning him to the balloon."

Cadmus felt his heels shove suddenly against the floor. He thought for a minute he hadn't heard straight. Then he knew he had, for the major had reached for a clean sheet of paper and dipped his pen. It was getting dark and the panes in the window had turned to mirrors and in one of them he could see himself standing with his mouth half open.

"Balloon?" he said.

General Johnston had started toward his desk. He stopped short and looked sharply at Cadmus.

"Did you say something, Mr. Henry?"

Cadmus swallowed.

"I said, 'Balloon,' sir."

"Well?" It was a cold word.

"I thought I was going to scout for you, sir. I don't know anything about balloons."

"Mr. Henry." The general raised himself slightly on his toes. His cheeks darkened. "I requested General Magruder to send me a qualified observer. You were assigned. You will accept the duty. Major Rhett will tell you when you are to make an ascent."

Cadmus said, "Yes, sir."

Major Rhett saw him out.

"It might be a good idea if you went to the balloon camp in the morning and had a talk with the crew. You'll have to learn about signals."

He spoke kindly and Cadmus said, "Yes, sir," like a grateful dog. Only he didn't actually feel grateful. He felt trapped.

The Federals had some balloons and whenever one of them went up, the Confederate gunners always tried to shoot it down. Cadmus remembered seeing one of them go up behind Wynn's Mill, and every Confederate cannon within range let go at it. One shell burst close enough to make the balloon rock crazily and Cadmus had cheered and laughed with the rest.

He realized now that that had been a wicked thing to do.

Cadmus found the balloon camp in an opening in the woods, about a half mile behind the lines. But he hadn't come to make any preliminary visit. He was going to go right up. And perhaps that was a good thing in a way, for he hadn't had time to get more than just about scared to death.

At six o'clock that morning he had been brought orders to report to General Johnston's headquarters. There Major Rhett had supplied him with notebook, pencils and a powerful pair of glasses. "We want you to mark down all the enemy troops you can see. Take your time, and identify them by organization, if possible. Estimate the numbers. Also mark down any moving troops, and any new batteries. You'll want to go high enough to get a look back as far as Howard's Bridge and Deep Creek." He dropped a hand on Cadmus's shoulder. "I'm sorry to call on you so suddenly. But you ought not to have any difficulty with signals and things. The crew has had experience. It would be a good idea though to keep the strap of those glasses round your neck all the time. They're valuable."

He shook hands.

"They'll be expecting you out there. Good luck, Mr. Henry."

It was an almost idyllic spot for a camp—that is, if you were camping there. The fine running spring, the stand of pine trees that left the ground free of underbrush and the good green grass meant nothing to Cadmus. All he saw was the apparatus that used up most of the open space.

It consisted of a long iron flue resting on bricks. One end of the flue was bent up and passed into the mouth of the balloon, while the bag, like the dead body of a slovenly monster, enclosed in the net of cordage, sprawled out on the grass beyond. A rope was attached to the cordage, from which it reached to an enormous windlass; it made several turns round the windlass and then continued off into the woods in coil after coil. To Cadmus's desperate eyes it did not seem possible that so much rope could exist in the world, let alone in the Confederate States of America.

The balloon crew must have heard him coming, for one of them was building a fire under the flue, while a round-shouldered Negro brought up pine knots and turpentine. The other men were standing near the windlass and they, with a fifth man, who appeared to have charge of the crew, watched Cadmus ride up.

The fifth man was a gangling individual with an intermittent flutter in his left eye. He was wearing what might have passed for a military cap at some earlier stage of its career.

"You Mr. Henry?" he inquired in a soft, slow voice.

Cadmus allowed he was.

"The boys will have her ready for you right quick," he said. "My name's Norment, Blaney Norment, Mr. Henry. I'm glad to be of service any time." His eyelid nearly closed and then slowly and fascinatingly fluttered open. "Mebane," he shouted, "you come here and take Mr. Henry's horse."

A second Negro came shuffling out of the woods, a little man with grizzled hair and a thin line of whiskers. When he saw the brown mare, his hands cupped a little, and he made a humming sound. The mare, who usually was leery of strangers, dropped her nose and made a faint whickering over the little man's head. When he led her off into the woods she went as slow and shuffling as he did.

"Something about Mebane," Norment said. "Horses like it. I don't know what it is."

Cadmus said something polite, but he didn't know what. He was watching the way the big Negro had begun slinging turpentine at the growing fire. The flames almost exploded upward and the roar of burning found an echo in the iron flue, as if the flames had hands to beat it with. He was conscious of the speculative stares of the men, but he didn't pay much attention. He was finding it hard to make his knees keep upright.

"That's a lot of rope, Mr. Norment," he said, because he had to say something.

"Maybe half a mile. It has good long splices. Mink makes good splices. He was a sailor."

The big Negro lifted his head. He looked at Cadmus briefly, and then threw another armful of knots on the fire. The man who had started the fire now came over to where Cadmus and Norment stood together. He looked like an Irishman and somewhere he had picked up a Zouave's red hat.

"She ought to start swelling pretty soon now, the danged old beast," he said, glancing at Cadmus from the corners of his eyes. "Will I get the gentleman the flag?"

"Yes," said Norment.

Neither he nor Cadmus had anything to say while the Irishman went for the flag. Cadmus wondered momentarily whether it was a Confederate flag, to be attached to the balloon. His attention was absorbed by a sudden swelling of the bag, just beyond the point where the flue entered it. It made no sound; or if it did, the roar of the fire covered it. He watched while the swelling grew. The fabric began to lift uncertainly, the center of heat shifting slightly as the draught through the flue gained or lost momentum. Whenever the last seemed to be the case, the Negro, Mink, threw on turpentine.

As the bag distended, Cadmus observed that it was made up of a great number of irregular pieces of cotton cloth, originally of varying colors, but now faded into an approximate uniformity. The cotton had been coated with some sort of waterproofing to make it airtight, but in places the coating had cracked, and the entire contrivance looked pretty dubious to Cadmus.

The Irishman returned with a small square of red bunting tacked onto a short stick. The man Norment took it from the Irishman.

"Here's the flag," he said. "When you want to go up, you wave up with it. When you want to go down, you wave down. It's easy to remember."

"How can you tell which way I'm waving?" Cadmus asked.

"Oh, we can figure it out," said Norment. "When a man wants to come down, he leans farther over the edge. Hooley, here, has good eyesight. Now when you're going up or going down, either one, and you want us to hurry up, you shake the flag. The more you want the boys to hurry, the harder you shake it. When you want us to leave off whatever we're doing, you wave."

Cadmus said, "I should think it would be plainer if you had two flags of different colors. That would tell you everything. Red to come down, blue to go up."

"We had a yellow one."

"What did you do with it?"

"Nothing. It got lost." Norment regarded him with a thoughtful expression. Suddenly his eyelid fluttered.

Cadmus looked away. The bag of the balloon was increasing enormously. Nearly free of the ground, it had definitely formed its spherical shape. Printed in huge letters around the side was the name *Pizzini*.

Seeing that Cadmus was looking at the name, Norment looked at it also.

"Was my brother," he explained. "That was his pro-

fessional name. Professor Pizzini. He dropped the flag and
tried to grab it."

Hooley said, "What goes up must come down." He
studied Cadmus out of the corners of his eyes.

Cadmus looked away. His feet didn't feel right. They
could have walked out from under him and he wouldn't
have known it.

Norment said, "I never sent up a balloon on this kind of
business. Only for my brother Pizzini, to make a civilized
ascent. Likely they'll shoot at you, Mr. Henry. Those Union
people over there, they shoot at anything. Shoot, shoot,
shoot, all day and all night till I get tired. But there's
one thing about it, they can't shoot only so high, so when
you get up far enough, they can't touch you. That's one
thing about it, all right."

Cadmus tried to grin.

"But you have to come back down through it."

"What goes up must come down," Hooley said again.

"You shut your mouth with that business," Norment told
him, in an utterly toneless voice. He walked over to the
windlass, and then back along the coils of rope. "You boys
got the end of that rope around something?"

They said no.

"You, Mink," Norment ordered, "you go tie that rope
around a tree. Can't never be sure about anything in
ballooning unless you're tied down to earth somewhere,"
he said to Cadmus. "Suppose a cannon shell dumped in
here and killed us all when she was still skin-full and hot—
that rope would ravel through that windlass like a tax
collector's soul. And the man up there wouldn't know a
thing about it till he found himself riding in the hand of
God. We don't want that to happen, Mr. Henry. There's a

time for all things. I guess the old bag's about ready for you."

Cadmus saw that it was so. The two men over by the windlass had laid hold of the handles and now the balloon had drawn free of the flue, and swung suddenly straight above the windlass, picking up its cords as it went. It poised there, a great sphere blotting out half the woods, a monstrous thing to grow in a quiet place, swinging a little, the cords slatting loosely together.

Norment respectfully touched his elbow.

"You want to get in right quick, Mr. Henry. The quicker you do that, the more hot air you've got to lift you."

"When will I know it's getting too cold?" Cadmus asked. "So I can signal you."

"You don't need to worry about that; we'll know."

"Yes," said Hooley, with his sidelong glance. "We'll know."

The Negro, Mink, came up to them. "Mist' No'ment, you all ready fo' de bahskit?" There was a peremptory note in his deep voice.

"When Mink says it's time to go, it is," Norment told Cadmus.

The suspension lines that connected the basket with the concentration ring tightened as the men at the windlass eased up on the brake handle. It seemed to Cadmus that he could see a tremor in the rope. He was conscious of the big Negro's glance, which was almost contemptuous. Mink's eyes seemed to take in everything, and it occurred to Cadmus that he probably had more to do with the actual management of the balloon than Norment.

"All right," he said. "I'm ready."

Mink turned a serious glance on him.

"Dat's good," he said. He steadied the basket with his great hands as Cadmus climbed in.

Cadmus stood holding onto one of the suspension lines with one hand, and grasping the small red flag in the other. He looked around on the good green grass and the line of woods from the shade of which the horses were watching him. The sunlight had a fine warmth. There was hardly a cloud in the sky. But he could feel the tremor in the great envelope as it came down through the net of cords into the suspension line his hand had hold of. He looked up and saw it over his head, looming against the blue sky like the belly of eternity. Underneath, the appendix, by which the hot air had entered this vastness, dangled incongruously, like an elephant's tail.

A slight jerk made him turn to see what the men at the windlass might be up to. But instead of the men, he saw the middle branches of the trees. The balloon was rising, and Cadmus was shocked to realize that he would have to look down if he wanted to see the clearing. The men at the windlass were working the handles; Norment had moved back, resting his hand on his narrow posterior and arching his back to look upward. His mouth was open. Hooley stood off to one side by himself and Mink was watching the uncoiling of the rope. It all seemed very simple and easy, now that he was underway. In fact, Cadmus thought, as he straightened himself in the narrow basket, there was practically nothing to it. He felt almost casual as he glanced out across the treetops.

Lee's house looked closer than he would have imagined. The line of the Warwick River came quickly into view. He made out the dams, the two mills and the Union earthworks on the far side. He could see the troops moving about behind them, the dark blue uniforms almost black, and the men standing on the ends of their shadows. Then he picked out a battery in a meadow beyond Dam No. 2. The guns were placed in a close line with the caissons close up. He could even see the battery teams in an elbow of the meadow, behind some trees. It gave him a curious feeling of detachment to look down on the enemy, as they went about their morning chores, oblivious of his eyes.

But then he noticed that men had started running to their guns. They looked to him like a smart outfit; and they must have had a serious alarm to react so sharply. He wondered what his own people might be up to. He couldn't see any signs of activity in the nearer woods, however, and he looked back at the battery to find an officer busily elevating one of the guns. The muzzle rose and kept on rising, and then it stopped, and Cadmus was seized by a horrid comprehension of the battery's excitement. They had seen the balloon. They were about to shoot at him.

A puff of smoke leaned out of the gun's muzzle and drew to one side, and in the same instant, it seemed to him, a shell burst on his left. In the next instant the entire surrounding sky was filled with bursting shells. They kept on bursting. He felt completely naked there, and tried instinctively to crouch down behind the basket rim; but the basket was made too small for that. He could neither sit nor kneel.

Then he remembered the red flag. It was still in his hand. Reaching out, he signalled frantically for speed and then ducked back again as a shell passed, cutting a kind of whistle out of the air. He shut his eyes and started praying and heard a thunderous explosion somewhere below. Then another, also below; and still another; and gradually he realized that all the bursts were below him.

But he couldn't get up or even open his eyes. He kept crouched as he was, with his heart hammering and a drenching sweat all over him.

A moment later the firing stopped entirely. He felt silence sweep over him, and when finally he opened his eyes, he was surrounded by the sky. Without looking down, he waved the flag from side to side to stop the ascent, and for a little he stayed still, just staring at the blue sky or at the bag over him, with its ridiculous, restless appendix. He had a strange and fanciful impression that the balloon, instead of being attached to earth by a straining rope, was suspended from some tackle in the sky. He could feel a stir of the air passing him. It was a little like resting in a fabulous swing.

His confidence came back to him with a rush. There was nothing those blue people could do to him now. As he thought of it, he came to the conclusion that none of their shells had burst anywhere really close. So he hoisted himself slightly and looked over the edge of the basket.

The Peninsula now lay like a cloth in gray and green and earth color, stitched and seamed with roads and rivers and fences. It was a clear and beautiful day. The lower waters of the James and the York were blue as the sky itself and to the east he saw the wide shine of the Bay.

All over the land below, and back toward Big Bethel, he made out units of enemy troops: some moving along the roads with what seemed infinite slowness; others in tented villages new-white on the green meadows. Houses and farm buildings cast bold shadows; and the shingled roofs of Yorktown were black and white. Three crows went by below, cocking their heads at him and raucously discussing this phenomenon of a man in the sky; and he had a sudden notion that perhaps they regarded his presence as a

usurpation of the rights of crows. It made him grin. He
pulled out his notebook and glasses and got to work.

It was a more difficult job than he had supposed, for no
sooner had he started sketching in Union positions, than
the balloon, with a kind of comic perversity, started
slowly to revolve; and Cadmus would no sooner have the
line of a field work started than it would have slipped past
the orbit of his vision. The basket was too narrow for him
to keep continually shifting, so that he had to wait till the
continuing revolution brought him round again. But he
had good eyes, and the crudely sketched map began to
fill up rapidly with the letters I or C or A, to indicate the
branches of the service, and the numerals beneath them
indicating Cadmus's estimate of their strength.

He had begun with the battery that had fired at him and
worked outward and eastward from that point. When
finally he finished his work, he turned his glasses back to
it again, and saw with a feeling of complete horror that
the Yankees had practically filled the field with guns.
There must have been three complete batteries brought
up while he was working, and more guns were struggling
through to roads for neighboring vantage points.

He leaned way over to look down at the balloon camp,
which now seemed very far away. He could not identify
the men from that distance, except for the Irishman,
Hooley, whose red cap stood out against the grass. But
when he turned the glasses on them, he saw all of them
looking upward, and the Irishman made a gesture with one
hand, as if he repeated his favorite phrase.

He had to go down, whether he liked to or not, for the
balloon would not retain its buoyancy indefinitely. He un-
furled the red flag and waved it.

Long before he reached the danger zone, single guns

had begun feeling out the range. The moment the balloon came low enough, the Yankees opened with all their batteries. The shells came in salvos; four, six and eight guns firing at once. Cadmus thought he could hear the shells rumbling from the instant of leaving the cannon's mouth until they burst. They burst in one continual, uninterrupted and enormous blast.

The balloon, which had started down with what had seemed to him a suicidal quickness, now hung floating with tantalizing slowness. He had once heard a minister with the preaching gift deliver what Great Uncle Eppa had pronounced a mighty sermon on the gaping jaws of hell. To Cadmus, the sounds and agonies described by that preacher were a trifle to what he was now passing through himself. He kept on signaling for more speed, and he said prayers at the top of his voice. And then, miraculously, he had passed through the thunder; he was behind the shelter of the trees; and the bombshells were passing overhead.

The balloon crew stood as they were, just staring at him, as if they didn't believe the evidence of their own eyes. The two men last at the windlass continued leaning on the handles. One of these was the Negro, Mink. His bowed shoulders were drenched with sweat and his chest labored heavily. But there was a kind of pride in his face as he looked at Cadmus, as if he now had a share in his existence.

"He wouldn't give up his handle, once you got in among them bombshells," Norment explained. "But the other boys took turns on the other one."

When Cadmus climbed out, the earth shifted under him and he had to hang onto the rim of the basket. A shivering was coming down the suspension lines. Looking up, he saw a puckering in the under side of the patchwork bag, as if the balloon too shared in the general exhaustion. Then abruptly the Yankees gave up shooting. Silence blanketed the clearing, and through the silence, shuffling slowly toward them and mumbling some kind of jargon about the Promised Land into her attentive ear, Mebane came leading the brown mare.

It was easier for Cadmus in the saddle. He looked down into the men's blank faces and tried to find some words to say to them. But he couldn't.

The flutter in Norment's eyelid was translated to the envelope of the balloon. It began to settle.

"We all wish you luck, Mr. Henry. Maybe we'll see you again some time. But it won't be this place, I reckon."

Norment looked regretfully round their comfortable camp site.

Cadmus tried to sound casual.

"I probably won't be going up again. But what makes you think you'll have to move?"

"Them Yankees," Norment said drearily. "Now they've missed the balloon, they'll be bound to try and hit us in this camp. Shoot, shoot, shoot. It makes me tired."

As if to second him, a Hotchkiss shell howled gaudily across the trees and exploded with a sudden thump a hundred yards or so back in the woods.

Jack Ellyat at Gettysburg

BY STEPHEN VINCENT BENÉT

Draw a clumsy fishhook now on a piece of paper,
To the left of the shank, by the bend of the curving hook,
Draw a Maltese cross with the top block cut away.
The cross is the town. Nine roads star out from it
East, West, South, North.
                    And now, still more to the left
Of the lopped-off cross, on the other side of the town,
Draw a long, slightly wavy line of ridges and hills
Roughly parallel to the fishhook shank.
(The hook of the fishhook is turned away from the cross
And the wavy line.)
                There your ground and your ridges lie.
The fishhook is Cemetery Ridge and the North

Waiting to be assaulted—the wavy line
Seminary Ridge whence the Southern assault will come.

The valley between is more than a mile in breadth.
It is some three miles from the lowest jut of the cross
To the button at the far end of the fishhook shank,
Big Round Top, with Little Round Top not far away.
Both ridges are strong and rocky, well made for war.
But the Northern one is the stronger shorter one.
Lee's army must spread out like an uncoiled snake
Lying along a fence rail, while Meade's can coil
Or halfway coil, like a snake part clung to a stone.
Meade has the more men and the easier shifts to make,
Lee the old prestige of triumph and his tried skill.
His task is—to coil his snake round the other snake
Halfway clung to the stone, and shatter it so,
Or to break some point in the shank of the fishhook line
And so cut the snake in two.
                              Meade's task is to hold.

That is the chess and the scheme of the wooden blocks
Set down on the contour map.
                              Having learned so much,
Forget it now, while the ripple lines of the map
Arise into bouldered ridges, tree-grown, bird-visited,
Where the gnats buzz, and the wren builds a hollow nest
And the rocks are gray in the sun and black in the rain,
And the jack-in-the-pulpits grow in the cool, damp hollows.
See no names of leaders painted upon the blocks
Such as "Hill," or "Hancock," or "Pender"—
                                        but see instead
Three miles of living men—three long double miles
Of men and guns and horses and fires and wagons,

Teamsters, surgeons, generals, orderlies,
A hundred and sixty thousand living men
Asleep or eating or thinking of writing brief
Notes in the thought of death, shooting dice or swearing,
Groaning in hospital wagons, standing guard
While the slow stars walk through heaven in silver mail,
Hearing a stream or a joke or a horse cropping grass
Or hearing nothing, being too tired to hear.
All night till the round sun comes and the morning breaks,
Three double miles of live men.
Listen to them, their breath goes up through the night
In a great chord of life, in the sighing murmur
Of wind-stirred wheat.
                        A hundred and sixty thousand
Breathing men, at night, on two hostile ridges set down.

Jack Ellyat slept that night on the rocky ground
Of Cemetery Hill while the cold stars marched,
And if his bed was harder than Jacob's stone
Yet he could sleep on it now and be glad for sleep.

He had been through Chancellorsville and the whistling
        wood,
He had been through this last day. It is well to sleep
After such days.
                        He had seen in the last four months
Many roads, much weather and death, and two men fey
Before they died with the prescience of death to come,
John Haberdeen and the corporal from Millerstown.
Such things are often remembered even in sleep.
He thought to himself, before he lay on the ground,
"We got it hot today in that red-brick town
But we'll get it hotter tomorrow."

And when he woke
And saw the round sun risen in the clear sky,
He could feel that thought steam up from the rocky ground
And touch each man.
One man looked down from the hill,
"That must be their whole damn army," he said and
    whistled,
"It'll be a picnic today, boys. Yes, it'll be
A regular basket-picnic." He whistled again.

"Shut your trap about picnics, Ace," said another man,
"You make me too damn hungry!"
He sighed out loud.
"We had enough of a picnic at Chancellorsville,"
He said. "I ain't felt right in my stummick since.
Can you make 'em out?"
"Sure," said Ace, "but they're pretty far."

"Wonder who we'll get? That bunch we got yesterday
Was a mean-shootin' bunch."
"Now don't you worry," said Ace.
"We'll get plenty."
The other man sighed again.
"Did you see that darky woman selling hot pies,
Two days ago, on the road?" he said, licking his lips,
"Blackberry pies. The boys ahead got a lot
And Jake and me clubbed together for three. And then
Just as we were ready to make the sneak,
Who comes up with a roar but the provost guard?
Did we get any pies? I guess you know if we did.
I couldn't spit for an hour, I felt so mad.
Next war I'm goin' to be provost guard or bust."

A thin voice said abruptly, "They're moving—lookit—
They're moving, I tell you—lookit—"
                              They all looked then.
A little crackling noise as of burning thornsticks
Began far away—ceased wholly—began again—
"We won't get it awhile," thought Ellyat. "They're trying
    the left.
We won't get it awhile, but we'll get it soon.
I feel funny today. I don't think I'm going to be killed
But I feel funny. That's their whole army all right.
I wonder if those other two felt like this,
John Haberdeen and the corporal from Millerstown?
What's it like to see your name on a bullet?
It must feel queer. This is going to be a big one.
The Johnnies know it. That house looks pretty down there.
Phaëton, charioteer in your drunken car,
What have you got for a man that carries my name?
We're a damn good company now, if we say it ourselves,
And the Old Man knows it—but this one's bound to be
    tough.

Charioteer, you were driving yesterday,
No doubt, but I did not see you. I see you now.
What have you got today for a man with my name?"

The firing began that morning at nine o'clock,
But it was three before the attacks were launched.
There were two attacks, one a drive on the Union left
To take the Round Tops, the other one on the right.
Lee had planned them to strike together and, striking so,
Cut the Union snake in three pieces.
                              It did not happen.

On the left, Dutch Longstreet, slow, pugnacious and
    stubborn,
Hard to beat and just as hard to convince,
Has his own ideas of the battle and does not move
For hours after the hour that Lee had planned,
Though, when he does, he moves with pugnacious strength.

Facing him, in the valley before the Round Tops,
Sickles thrusts out blue troops in a weak right angle,
Some distance from the Ridge, by the Emmettsburg pike.
There is a peach orchard there, a field of ripe wheat
And other peaceable things soon not to be peaceful.

They say the bluecoats, marching through the ripe wheat,
Made a blue-and-yellow picture that men remember
Even now in their age, in their crack-voiced age.
They say the noise was incessant as the sound
Of all wolves howling, when that attack came on.
They say, when the guns all spoke, that the solid ground
Of the rocky ridges trembled like a sick child.
We have made the sick earth tremble with other shakings
In our time, in our time, in our time, but it has not taught
    us
To leave the grain in the field.
                        So the storm came on
Yelling against the angle.
                    The men who fought there
Were the tired fighters, the hammered, the weather-
    beaten, the very hard-dying men.
                            They came and died
And came again and died and stood there and died,
Till at last the angle was crumpled and broken in,

Sickles shot down, Willard, Barlow and Semmes shot
    down,
Wheatfield and orchard bloody and trampled and taken,
And Hood's tall Texans sweeping on toward the Round
    Tops
As Hood fell wounded.
                      On Little Round Top's height
Stands a lonely figure, seeing that rush come on—
Greek-mouthed Warren, Meade's chief of engineers.
—Sometimes, and in battle even, a moment comes
When a man with eyes can see a dip in the scales
And, so seeing, reverse a fortune. Warren has eyes
And such a moment comes to him now. He turns
—In a clear flash seeing the crests of the Round Tops
    taken, the gray artillery there and the battle lost—
And rides off hell-for-leather to gather troops
And bring them up in the very nick of time,
While the gray rush still advances, keening its cry.
The crest is three times taken and then retaken
In fierce wolf-flurries of combat, in gasping Iliads
Too rapid to note or remember, too obscure to freeze in a
    song.
But at last, when the round sun drops, when the nun-
    footed night,
Dark-veiled walker, holding the first weak stars
Like children against her breast, spreads her pure cloths
    there,
The Union still holds the Round Tops and the two hard
    keys of war.

Night falls. The blood drips in the rocks of the Devil's Den.
The murmur begins to rise from the thirsty ground
Where the twenty thousand dead and wounded lie.

Such was Longstreet's war, and such the Union defence,
The deaths and the woundings, the victory and defeat
At the end of the fishhook shank.

                        And so Longstreet failed
Ere Ewell and Early struck the fishhook itself
At Culp's Hill and the Ridge and at Cemetery Hill,
With better fortune, though not with fortune enough
To plant hard triumph deep on the sharp-edged rocks
And break the scales of the snake.

                            When that last attack
Came, with its cry, Jack Ellyat saw it come on.

They had been waiting for hours on that hard hill,
Sometimes under fire, sometimes untroubled by shells.
A man chewed a stick of grass and hummed to himself.
Another played mumbledeypeg with a worn black knife.
Two men were talking girls till they got too mad
And the sergeant stopped them.

                          Then they waited again.

Jack Ellyat waited, hearing that other roar.
Rise and fall, be distant and then approach.
Now and then he turned on his side and looked at the sky
As if to build a house of peace from that blue,
But could find no house of peace there.

                          Only the roar,
The slow sun sinking, the fey touch at his mind . . .

He was lying behind a tree and a chunk of rock
On thick, coarse grass. Farther down the slope of the hill
There were houses, a rough stone wall, and blue loungy
    men.
Behind them lay the batteries on the crest.

He wondered if there were people still in the houses.
One house had a long, slant roof. He followed the slant
Of the roof with his finger, idly, pleased with the line.

The shelling burst out from the Southern guns again.
Their own batteries answered behind them. He looked at
    his house
While the shells came down. I'd like to live in that house.
Now the shelling lessened.
                      The man with the old black knife
Shut up the knife and began to baby his rifle.
They're coming, Jack thought. This is it.
                           There was an abrupt
Slight stiffening in the bodies of other men,
A few chopped ends of words scattered back and forth,
Eyes looking, hands busy in swift, well-accustomed
    gestures.
This is it. He felt his own hands moving like theirs
Though he was not telling them to. This is it. He felt
The old familiar tightness around his chest.
The man with the grass chewed his stalk a little too hard
And then suddenly spat it out.
                      Jack Ellyat saw
Through the falling night, that slight, gray fringe that was
    war
Coming against them, not as it came in pictures
With a ruler-edge, but a crinkled and smudgy line
Like a child's vague scrawl in soft crayon, but moving on,
But with its little red handkerchiefs of flags
Sagging up and down, here and there.
                      It was still quite far,
It was still like a toy attack—it was swallowed now
By a wood and came out larger with larger flags.

Their own guns on the crest were trying to break it up
—Smoking sand thrown into an ant-legged line—
But it still kept on—one fringe and another fringe
And another and—
                        He lost them all for a moment
In a dip of ground.
                        That is it, he thought with a parched
Mind. It's a big one. They must be yelling all right
Though you can't hear them. They're going to do it this
        time,
Do it or bust—you can tell from the way they come—
I hope to Christ that the batteries do their job
When they get out of that dip.
                        Hell, they've lost 'em now,
And they're still coming.
                        He heard a thin gnat-shrieking
"Hold your fire till they're close enough, men!"
                        The new lieutenant.
The new lieutenant looked thin. "Aw, go home," he
        muttered,
"We're no militia— What do you think we are?"

Then suddenly, down by his house, the low stone wall
Flashed and was instantly huge with a wall of smoke.
He was yelling now. He saw a red battle flag
Push through smoke like a prow and be blotted out
By smoke and flash.
                        His heart knocked hard in his chest.
"Do it or bust," he mumbled, holding his fire
While the rags of smoke blew off.
                        He heard a thick chunk
Beside him, turned his head for a flicker of time.

The man who had chewed on the grass was injuredly
    trying
To rise on his knees, his face annoyed by a smile.
Then the blood poured over the smile and he crumpled up.
Ellyat stretched out a hand to touch him and felt the hand
Rasped by a file.
                        He jerked back the hand and sucked it.
"Bastards," he said in a minor and even voice.

All this had occurred, it seemed, in no time at all,
But when he turned back, the smoky slope of the hill
Was gray—and a staggering red advancing flag
And those same shouting strangers he knew so well,
No longer ants—but there—and stumblingly running—
And that high, shrill, hated keen piercing all the flat
    thunder.

His lips went back. He felt something swell in his chest
Like a huge, indocile bubble.
                        "By God," he said,
Loading and firing. "You're not going to get this hill,
You're not going to get this hill. By God, but you're not!"

He saw one gray man spin like a crazy dancer
And another fall at his heels—but the hill kept growing
    them.
Something made him look toward his left.
                        A yellow-fanged face
Was aiming a pistol over a chunk of rock.
He fired and the face went down like a broken pipe
While something hit him sharply and took his breath.
"Get back, you suckers," he croaked. "Get back there, you
    suckers!"

He wouldn't have time to load now—they were too near.
He was up and screaming. He swung his gun like a club
Through a twilight full of bright stabbings, and felt it
    crash
On a thing that broke. He had no breath any more.
He had no thoughts. Then the blunt fist hit him again.

He was down in the grass and the black sheep of night ran
    over him . . .

The Battleground

BY ELSIE SINGMASTER

Mercifully, Mary Bowman, a widow, whose husband had been missing since the battle of Gettysburg, had been warned, together with other citizens of Gettysburg, that on Thursday the nineteenth of November, 1863, she would be awakened from sleep by a bugler's reveille, and that during that great day she would hear again the dread sound of cannon.

Nevertheless, hearing again the reveille, she sat up in bed with a scream and put her hands over her ears. Then, gasping, groping about in her confusion and terror, she rose and began to dress. She put on a dress which had been once a bright plaid, but which now, having lost both its color and the stiff, outstanding quality of the skirts of

'63, hung about her in straight and dingy folds. It was clean, but it had upon it certain ineradicable brown stains on which soap and water seemed to have had no effect. She was thin and pale, and her eyes had a set look, as though they saw other sights than those directly about her.

In the bed from which she had risen lay her little daughter; in a trundle bed near by, her two sons, one about ten years old, the other about four. They slept heavily, lying deep in their beds, as though they would never move. Their mother looked at them with her strange, absent gaze; then she barred a little more closely the broken shutters, and went down the stairs. The shutters were broken in a curious fashion. Here and there they were pierced by round holes, and one hung from a single hinge. The window frames were without glass, the floor was without carpet, the beds without pillows.

In her kitchen Mary Bowman looked about her as though still seeing other sights. Here, too, the floor was carpetless. Above the stove a patch of fresh plaster on the wall showed where a great rent had been filled in; in the doors were the same little round holes as in the shutters of the room above. But there was food and fuel, which was more than one might have expected from the aspect of the house and its mistress. She opened the shattered door of the cupboard, and, having made the fire, began to prepare breakfast.

Outside the house there was already, at six o'clock, noise and confusion. Last evening a train from Washington had brought to the village Abraham Lincoln; for several days other trains had been bringing less distinguished guests, until thousands thronged the little town. This morning the tract of land between Mary Bowman's house and the village cemetery was to be dedicated for the burial of the

Union dead, who were to be laid there in sweeping semi-circles round a center on which a great monument was to rise.

But of the dedication, of the President of the United States, of his distinguished associates, of the great crowds, of the soldiers, of the crape-banded banners, Mary Bowman and her children would see nothing. Mary Bowman would sit in her little wrecked kitchen with her children. For to her the President of the United States and others in high places who prosecuted war or who tolerated war, who called for young men to fight, were hateful. To Mary Bowman the crowds of curious persons who coveted a sight of the great battlefields were ghouls; their eyes wished to gloat upon ruin, upon fragments of the weapons of war, upon torn bits of the habiliments of soldiers; their feet longed to sink into the loose ground of hastily made graves; the discovery of a partially covered body was precious to them.

Mary Bowman knew that field! From Culp's Hill to the McPherson farm, from Big Round Top to the poorhouse, she had traveled it, searching, searching, with frantic, insane disregard of positions or of possibility. Her husband could not have fallen here among the Eleventh Corps, he could not lie here among the unburied dead of the Louisiana Tigers! If he was in the battle at all, it was at the Angle that he fell.

She had not been able to begin her search immediately after the battle because there were forty wounded men in her little house; she could not prosecute it with any diligence even later, when the soldiers had been carried to the hospitals, in the Presbyterian Church, the Catholic Church, the two Lutheran churches, the Seminary, the

College, the Courthouse, and the great tented hospital on the York road. Nurses were here, Sisters of Mercy were here, compassionate women were here by the score; but still she was needed, with all the other women of the village, to nurse, to bandage, to comfort, to pray with those who must die. Little Mary Bowman had assisted at the amputation of limbs, she had helped to control strong men torn by the frenzy of delirium, she had tended poor bodies which had almost lost all semblance to humanity. Neither she nor any of the other women of the village counted themselves especially heroic; the delicate wife of the judge, the petted daughter of the doctor, the gently bred wife of the preacher forgot that fainting at the sight of blood was one of the distinguishing qualities of their sex; they turned back their sleeves and repressed their tears, and, shoulder to shoulder with Mary Bowman and her Irish neighbor, Hannah Casey, they fed the hungry and healed the sick and clothed the naked. If Mary Bowman had been herself, she might have laughed at the sight of her dresses cobbled into trousers, her skirts wrapped round the shoulders of sick men. But neither then nor ever after did Mary laugh at any incident of that summer.

Hannah Casey laughed, and by and by she began to boast. Meade, Hancock, Slocum, were noncombatants beside her. She had fought whole companies of Confederates, she had wielded bayonets, she had assisted at the spiking of a gun, she was Barbara Frietchie and Molly Pitcher combined. But all her lunacy could not make Mary Bowman smile.

Of John Bowman no trace could be found. No one could tell her anything about him, to her frantic letters no one responded. Her old friend, the village judge, wrote letters also, but could get no reply. Her husband was missing; it was probable that he lay somewhere upon this field, the field upon which they had wandered as lovers.

In midsummer a few trenches were opened, and Mary, unknown to her friends, saw them opened. At the uncovering of the first great pit, she actually helped with her own hands. For those of this generation who know nothing of war, that fact may be written down, to be passed over lightly. The soldiers, having been on other battlefields, accepted her presence without comment. She did not cry, she only helped doggedly, and looked at what they found. That, too, may be written down for a generation which has not known war.

Immediately, an order went forth that no graves, large or small, were to be opened before cold weather. The citizens were panic-stricken with fear of an epidemic; already there were many cases of dysentery and typhoid. Now that the necessity for daily work for the wounded was past, the village became nervous, excited, irritable. Several men and boys were killed while trying to open unexploded shells; their deaths added to the general horror. There were constant visitors who sought husbands, brothers, sweethearts; with these the Gettysburg women were still able to weep, for them they were still able to care; but the constant demand for entertainment for the curious annoyed those who wished to be left alone to recover from the shock of battle. Gettysburg was prostrate, bereft of many of its worldly possessions, drained to the bottom of its well of sympathy. Its schools must be opened, its poor must be helped. Cold weather was coming and there were many, like Mary Bowman, who owned no longer any quilts or blankets, who had given away their clothes, their linen, even the precious sheets which their grandmothers had spun. Gettysburg grudged nothing, wished nothing back, it asked only to be left in peace.

When the order was given to postpone the opening of graves till fall, Mary began to go about the battlefield searching alone. Her good, obedient children stayed at home in the house or in the little field. They were beginning to grow thin and wan, they were shivering in the hot August weather, but their mother did not see. She gave them a great deal more to eat than she had herself, and they had far better clothes than her bloodstained motley.

She went about the battlefield with her eyes on the ground, her feet treading gently, anticipating loose soil or some sudden obstacle. Sometimes she stooped suddenly. To fragments of shells, to bits of blue or gray cloth, to cartridge belts or broken muskets, she paid no heed; at sight of pitiful bits of human bodies she shuddered. But there lay also upon that field little pocket Testaments, letters, trinkets, photographs. John had had her photograph and the children's, and surely he must have had some of the letters she had written!

But poor Mary found nothing.

One morning, late in August, she sat beside her kitchen table with her head on her arm. The first of the scarlet gum leaves had begun to drift down from the shattered trees; it would not be long before the ground would be covered, and those depressed spots, those tiny wooden headstones, those fragments of blue and gray be hidden. The thought smothered her. She did not cry, she had not cried at all. Her soul seemed hardened, stiff, like the terrible wounds for which she had helped to care.

Suddenly, hearing a sound, Mary had looked up. The judge stood in the doorway; he had known all about her since she was a little girl; something in his face told her that he knew also of her terrible search. She did not ask him to sit down, she said nothing at all. She had been a loquacious person, she had become an abnormally silent one. Speech hurt her.

The judge looked round the little kitchen. The rent in the wall was still unmended, the chairs were broken; there was nothing else to be seen but the table and the rusty stove and the thin, friendless-looking children standing by the door. It was the house not only of poverty and woe, but of neglect.

"Mary," said the judge, "how do you mean to live?"

Mary's thin, sunburned hand stirred a little as it lay on the table.

"I do not know."

"You have these children to feed and clothe and you must furnish your house again. Mary—" The judge hesitated for a moment. John Bowman had been a school-teacher, a thrifty, ambitious soul, who would have thought it a disgrace for his wife to earn her living. The judge laid his hand on the thin hand beside him. "Your children must have food, Mary. Come down to my house, and my wife will give you work. Come now."

Slowly Mary had risen from her chair, and smoothed down her dress and obeyed him. Down the street they went together, seeing fences still prone, seeing walls torn by shells, past the houses where the shock of battle had hastened the deaths of old persons and little children, and had disappointed the hearts of those who longed for a child, to the judge's house in the square. There wagons stood about, loaded with wheels of cannon, fragments of burst caissons, or with long, narrow pine boxes, brought from the railroad, to be stored against the day of exhumation. Men were laughing and shouting to one another, the driver of the wagon on which the long boxes were piled cracked his whip as he urged his horses.

Hannah Casey congratulated her neighbor heartily upon her finding work.

"That'll fix you up," she assured her.

She visited Mary constantly, she reported to her the news of the war, she talked at length of the coming of the President.

"I'm going to see him," she announced. "I'm going to shake him by the hand. I'm going to say, 'Hello, Abe, you old rail splitter, God bless you!' Then the bands'll play, and the people will march, and the Johnny Rebs will hear 'em in their graves."

Mary Bowman put her hands over her ears.

"I believe in my soul you'd let 'em all rise from the dead!"

"I would!" said Mary Bowman hoarsely. "I would!"

"Well, not so Hannah Casey! Look at me garden tore to bits! Look at me beds, stripped to the ropes!"

And Hannah Casey departed to her house.

Details of the coming celebration penetrated to the ears of Mary Bowman whether she wished it or not, and the gathering crowds made themselves known. They stood upon her porch, they examined the broken shutters, they wished to question her. But Mary Bowman would answer no questions, would not let herself be seen. To her the thing was horrible. She saw the battling hosts, she heard once more the roar of artillery, she smelled the smoke of battle, she was torn by its confusion. Besides, she seemed to feel in the ground beneath her a feebly stirring, suffering, ghastly host. They had begun again to open the trenches, and she looked into them.

Now, on the morning of Thursday, the nineteenth of November, her children dressed themselves and came down the steps. They had begun to have a little plumpness and color, but the dreadful light in their mother's eyes was still reflected in theirs. On the lower step they hesitated, looking at the door. Outside stood the judge, who had found time in the multiplicity of his cares, to come to the little house.

He spoke with kind but firm command.

"Mary," said he, "you must take these children to hear President Lincoln."

"What!" cried Mary.

"You must take these children to the exercises."

"I cannot!" cried Mary. "I cannot! I cannot!"

"You must!" The judge came into the room. "Let me hear no more of this going about. You are a Christian, your husband was a Christian. Do you want your children to think it is a wicked thing to die for their country? Do as I tell you, Mary."

Mary got up from her chair, and put on her children all the clothes they had, and wrapped about her own shoulders a little black coat which the judge's wife had given her. Then, as one who steps into an unfriendly sea, she started out with them into the great crowd. Once more, poor Mary said to herself, she would obey. She had seen the platform; by going round through the citizen's cemetery she could get close to it.

The November day was bright and warm, but Mary and her children shivered. Slowly she made her way close to the platform, patiently she stood and waited. Sometimes she stood with shut eyes, swaying a little. On the moonlit night of the third day of battle she had ventured from her house down toward the square to try to find some brandy for the dying men about her, and as in a dream she had

seen a tall general, mounted upon a white horse with muffled hoofs, ride down the street. Bending from his saddle
he had spoken, apparently to the empty air.

"Up, boys, up!"

There had risen at his command thousands of men lying
asleep on pavement and street, and quietly, in an intermi-
nable line, they had stolen out like dead men toward the
Seminary, to join their comrades and begin the long, long
march to Hagerstown. It seemed to her that all about her
dead men might rise now to look with reproach upon these
strangers who disturbed their rest.

The procession was late, the orator of the day was de-
layed, but still Mary waited, swaying a little in her place.
Presently the great guns roared forth a welcome, the bands
played, the procession approached. On horseback, erect,
gauntleted, the President of the United States drew rein
beside the platform, and, with the orator and the other
famous men, dismounted. There were great cheers, there
were deep silences, there were fresh volleys of artillery,
there was new music.

Of it all, Mary Bowman heard but little. Remembering
the judge, whom she saw now near the President, she tried
to obey the spirit as well as the letter of his command; she
directed her children to look, she turned their heads toward the platform.

Men spoke and prayed and sang, and Mary stood still
in her place. The orator of the day described the battle,
he eulogized the dead, he proved the righteousness of this
great war; his words fell upon Mary's ears unheard. If she
had been asked who he was, she might have said vaguely
that he was Mr. Lincoln. When he ended, she was ready to
go home. There was singing; now she could slip away,

through the gaps in the cemetery fence. She had done as the judge commanded and now she would go back to her house.

With her arms about her children, she started away. Then someone who stood near by took her by the hand.

"Madam," said he, "the President is going to speak!"

Half turning, Mary looked back. The thunder of applause made her shiver, made her even scream, it was so like that other thunderous sound which she would hear forever. She leaned upon her little children heavily, trying to get her breath, gasping, trying to keep her consciousness. She fixed her eyes upon the rising figure before her, she clung to the sight of him as a drowning swimmer in deep waters, she struggled to fix her thoughts upon him. Exhaustion, grief, misery threatened to engulf her, she hung upon him in desperation.

Slowly, as one who is old or tired or sick at heart, he rose to his feet, the President of the United States, the Commander in Chief of the Army and Navy, the hope of his country. Then he stood waiting. In great waves of sound the applause rose and died and rose again. He waited quietly. The winner of debate, the great champion of a great cause, the veteran in argument, the master of men, he looked down upon the throng. The clear, simple things he had to say were ready in his mind, he had thought them out, written out a first draft of them in Washington, copied it here in Gettysburg. It is probable that now, as he waited to speak, his mind traveled to other things, to the misery, the wretchedness, the slaughter of this field, to the tears of mothers, the grief of widows, the orphaning of little children.

Slowly, in his clear voice, he said what little he had to say. To the weary crowd, settling itself into position once more, the speech seemed short; to the cultivated who had been listening to the elaborate periods of great oratory, it seemed commonplace, it seemed a speech which anyone might have made. But it was not so with Mary Bowman, nor with many other unlearned persons. Mary Bowman's soul seemed to smooth itself out like a scroll, her hands lightened their clutch on her children, the beating of her heart slackened, she gasped no more.

She could not have told exactly what he said, though later she read it and learned it and taught it to her children and her children's children. She only saw him, felt him, breathed him in, this great, common, kindly man. His gaze seemed to rest upon her; it was not impossible, it was even probable, that during the hours that passed he had singled out that little group so near him, that desolate woman in her motley dress, with her children clinging about her. He said that the world would not forget this field, these martyrs; he said it in words which Mary Bowman could understand, he pointed to a future for which there was a new task.

"Daughter!" he seemed to say to her from the depths of trouble, of responsibility, of care greater than her own. "Daughter, be of good comfort!"

Unhindered now, amid the cheers, across ground which seemed no longer to stir beneath her feet, Mary Bowman went back to her house. There, opening the shutters, she bent and solemnly kissed her little children, saying to herself that henceforth they must have more food and raiment; they must be given some joy in life.

The Day After Thanksgiving

BY HARNETT T. KANE

In a simple white house with four narrow wooden columns at the front and log cabins in the yard, there was a nervous stir during November of 1863. As the early morning mists rose from Stewart's Creek at the base of the hilly plateau, the Davises and their younger children were talking of their hopes. Perhaps the situation might change and son Sam would come home, after all, if only for a little while . . .

Nobody at the Davis farm in the rolling green foothills of middle Tennessee spoke much about Sam's army work. With the Union forces so close around them, it was not a subject to be discussed, even among friends. From Nashville, only fifteen miles away, rumors had arisen of trouble down in Chattanooga, where a great battle could break out at any time. But one or two relatives whispered that Sam and his fellow scouts had been seen somewhere near the farm only a day or two ago.

Sam's mother, her hair slightly grayed, might not have found this good news. She worried over her twenty-one-year-old son, even though his superior was their good friend, Captain Shaw. She had been sorry that Sam agreed to join Shaw's scouting service. Still, they should consider it fortunate that Henry Shaw, and not a complete stranger, had charge of Sam's work. For that, at least, the Davises might be grateful in this Thanksgiving month.

For weeks the Union spy director, General Grenville Dodge, had fretted. For all his energetic efforts, a band of Confederate scouts was moving within Northern lines and gathering alarmingly accurate information. In early November General U. S. Grant's powerful army faced that of the Southerner Bragg at Chattanooga, with the green majesty of Lookout Mountain as a backdrop. A decision was close, and few knew it better than Grenville Dodge.

With his headquarters in the middle area of Tennessee, Dodge worried as each day brought new reports of the damaging presence of the Confederate scouts. They slipped in and out of Nashville, in the open country and along back roads so familiar to these Tennessee natives. Several had been detected among Dodge's own forces.

The Union general gave orders to his own spies and scouts to wipe out the Confederate agents, to arrest anybody who was the least suspicious or who could not offer a clear explanation of his reasons for being there. In particular Dodge wanted to get a shadowy individual whom the Federal Army appeared to know only by the assumed name of E. C. Coleman, sometimes a soldier, more often a civilian—an "herb specialist," this Dr. Coleman. There was a substantial reward out for him, preferably alive, though a dead Coleman would also be acceptable.

Captain Henry Shaw (Coleman), a man of several names and identities, left a trail through Union territory, but it was a thin one, a ghostlike thread. If the Federals could just once identify and lay hands on him! The Davis family of that mid-State farm had been Henry Shaw's friends for years, during his schoolteacher days and his time as a steamboat clerk. Shaw was an outstanding fellow with an imposing physique, tall and robust. His bright blue eyes were keenly observant, his nose was sharp, and he had a small reddish beard. He had considerable self-possession, a look of quiet assurance—an assurance that was to undergo the supreme test of his life. There would be another kind of testing for the Davises.

Young Sam Davis had spent most of his days on the family farm a mile outside Smyrna, Tennessee. The first of eight children, with three older half brothers and a half sister, he had been accustomed to horseback rides and hunting through the woods of the country—the usual life of the country boy. By all accounts, the sixty-three-year-old father was upright, undemonstrative, some said stern; Sam's mother, who was only forty, had a soft and gentle manner, shared to a degree by her eldest son. The boy had always been close to her. When he left to attend Western Military Institute at Nashville, neighbors and friends thought that Sam suffered a special homesickness; as often as he could, he returned to see his mother.

Yet Sam fitted in at school, adapting to the discipline, liking it. He had started at the Institute when he was eighteen, in 1860; a year later, at the outbreak of war, Sam and his schoolmates marched off to join the Rutherford Rifles, 1st Regiment, Tennessee Volunteer Infantry. As his father ultimately told the proud story of Sam's career, he first tasted fire at Cheat Mountain in western Virginia, under the command of Robert E. Lee. Then, in Stonewall Jackson's brigade, he helped push the Union army across the Potomac during the harsh winter of 1862.

Next Sam was called back to Tennessee with his fellows. Bad times had come to the West; under Johnston and Beauregard the youth had known the violence and tragedy of Shiloh, where he suffered battle wounds. Then, in the days of scant arms and reduced rations, Braxton Bragg had taken command of the Army of Tennessee. Quickly Bragg approved the formation of a new company of scouts to be his "eyes and ears" and find out what the Federals intended to do.

Sam Davis's friend Shaw was recruiting scouts and Sam volunteered. He looked younger than his twenty years, tall, with a lean body, dark brown hair, and a skin well tanned by years in the sun. He had a mustache but, unlike most soldiers, no beard. He was not talkative, and his manner had a suggestion of shyness. But Captain Henry Shaw needed no recommendation; he had seen Sam under fire, and he accepted him at once. For months Sam had served efficiently and quietly, and Shaw's respect had increased with each assignment.

In the fall of 1863, Captain Shaw and his scouts had to try to get all available information about Union operations at Nashville and at Dodge's headquarters in the town of Pulaski, to be dispatched to the battle headquarters of General Bragg. The shadowy Shaw conferred from day to day with his group, gathering their reports, comparing the facts that they brought him.

One agent went into Nashville in country clothes, driving a wagon filled with firewood, and mingling with towns-people and soldiers. Another, in neat civilian dress, attended a dance in a town near Union headquarters, arriving late, listening carefully to the privates' conversation, leaving early before the question was raised of his identity. The adroit Shaw had long ago learned another device, the trick of placing his agents at fixed points along a Union line of march. For forty-eight hours or longer each vantage point—a clump of bushes, a large boulder—would be manned, and a definite count made by trained soldiers.

This time the Confederate scouts had a windfall, in a source of information close to Dodge's own headquarters. According to a native, a good-looking Tennessee girl "beguiled" one of the general's young officers. Another insisted that a Negro porter picked up documents from a table, sought out a Confederate who employed his wife, and gave them over. Whatever the explanation, the papers were accurate, so accurate that the Union general felt utter dismay when he came upon them at a later date.

For Shaw and his scouts a deadline approached; in a few days all of this information must be unified and sent to Bragg, and the men would start for Chattanooga, separately or in small groups. It was their custom to have all documents carried by one of the party. If any of the others were caught, there would be no evidence against them; if the enemies trapped the carrier, only one man would be in danger. For this vital role Shaw picked Sam Davis, who looked like a schoolboy but had shown himself perhaps the most dependable of the lot.

Within twenty-four hours the group would meet again. Meanwhile Sam had great good fortune—permission to go home if he wished. Union soldiers had camped scarcely a mile from the Davis farm, but he could get through on a black night. So on a chill fall evening the boy rode stealthily toward the farmhouse. Tying his horse behind a big rock, he made his way across the lawn and tapped lightly at a window.

His tall father opened the door and Mrs. Davis ran out. Sam took his mother in his arms, shook his father's hand, and a few minutes later explained that he had only a little time, but he had wanted to see them. No, they mustn't wake the youngest girls, sleeping in a trundle bed; they should cover the windows and keep the lights low. Nobody else must know he had come. As he spoke, his mother touched his hand, asked questions, examined him with loving eyes.

Though there would later be confused descriptions of his dress, Sam Davis wore gray, washed-out Confederate trousers, a light nondescript jacket, and, it appeared, hat and top boots from a captured Union uniform. Hardpressed Southerners frequently used any Yankee garb that fell into their hands. The boy shivered slightly; Mrs. Davis saw that he needed a coat, and she remembered one of Union Blue, with cape, that he had once left at the house.

She had prepared it for him, dyeing it a vague brown. Using butternut or white walnut, the only coloring available, she had succeeded in making the garment an in-between shade. "Boy, you've got to take it," she told him. He agreed, and meanwhile his father stared at Sam's broken shoe. "Here, let me fix that one," he urged. As Mr. Davis worked, Sam lay down to rest for an hour or two.

Early in the morning his mother shook him and held the big coat for him. They waved from the door as he rode off.

He might not be with them for Thanksgiving, and still they could be thankful. They had seen their boy again, and he was alive and well.

In the home of a friend near Dodge's own quarters at Pulaski, young Sam met his chief. He went early to bed the next night, but Captain Shaw stayed up for hours, working over his reports. Not until dawn did he finish, and then he signaled that he had everything in order. Rising, Sam shook hands, swallowed a half cupful of weak wartime coffee, took the reports, and left.

He made good time, using lightly traveled roads. On November 20, on Lambs' ferry road in Giles County, men in blue sprang out of ambush and surrounded him. They were members of the 7th Kansas Cavalry, the so-called "Jayhawkers" who had been sent out to catch Shaw's scouts.

Soon afterward a Union officer asked him to take off his shoes. In silence Sam Davis removed them, and from a hollow beneath the sole a Northern soldier drew several sheets of paper, including a letter from "Coleman" to Bragg with full details of Federal troops, locations, intentions. Another soldier entered and displayed what he'd come across in the saddle—a full map and description of Nashville's newest fortifications.

The prisoner said nothing, and he was taken to the well-guarded county jail at Pulaski. Already it held about twenty-five other men, picked up on Dodge's order on varying degrees of suspicion. Sam recognized three of his fellow scouts, among them an older man with a reddish beard and a certain assurance.

The Federals had captured the Confederate they wanted most, for whom they had offered their large reward—the brilliant Captain Shaw himself. But they had no idea of his identity; they had picked him up as one of many civilians who had thus far not explained their presence in the area. The only person on whom evidence had been discovered was Sam himself.

Henry Shaw did not talk or signal to Sam. There was no need; the boy understood that no matter what happened in the days ahead, he was to give no sign that he had ever met him before. General Dodge went over the papers, and he was much disturbed. There was a traitor at his own headquarters, and he had to find who it was! He glared at the name of Coleman, chief of Bragg's scouts, on the letter Sam had carried. The man had signed it only a short time before; he must be nearby, and surely the boy knew where.

General Dodge had the prisoner brought to him. "Davis met me modestly," he recalled afterward. "He was a fine, soldierly looking young fellow, not over twenty. He had a frank, open face and was bright." The general spoke seriously.

"I tried to impress on him the danger he was in, and told him that I knew he was only a messenger, and urged him, on the promise of lenient treatment, to divulge the source of all the information."

Politely Sam shook his head. "That's something I won't tell, sir."

The general went on. Here the prisoner was, in Federal lines, wearing portions of Union costume, with damaging papers about Federal strength, written from one Confederate official to another. Didn't Sam see how damning that was? Surely he understood enough about Army rules to realize what would happen if he went before a court-martial. Let him help them in finding the man Coleman.

The boy bowed his head; he had nothing more to say.

With a sign Dodge summoned the guard. The general still had hope of locating Coleman by his own efforts. When he wrote General Sherman, forwarding a copy of Sam's messages, he noted: "Captain Coleman is pretty well posted. I think we will have him in a day or two."

Two days passed, and the Union soldiers reported failure in their hunt. Meanwhile Sam continued in jail with Coleman and the other scouts a few feet away; none of them betrayed themselves. Years afterward General Dodge disclosed that he placed in the jail "one of our own spies," who assured the prisoners that he was a good Confederate. They sensed the scheme at once, "and we obtained no information of value from them."

The Federal officers talked to Sam at length. The infantry chaplain, James Young of the 81st Ohio, spoke with him for a long time, as did the provost marshal and the leader of Dodge's scouts. They used varying tactics, blustering, threatening, pleading; he told them nothing.

One of the Confederate scouts said afterwards that each time Sam left the jail Captain Shaw watched anxiously, trying to hide his emotion. Would the boy be browbeaten into an admission, or trapped by an accidental answer? Over and over his captors asked Sam: Where was his chief, Coleman? When had he last seen him?

General Dodge, speaking as earnestly as he could, asked him to "give me a chance to save his life." Sam behaved more coolly than the man who had power over him: "I won't tell, General. You're doing your duty as a soldier, and I'll do mine, if I have to die."

Sam was the same age as the sons of many of the officers; with each day he impressed them more favorably. Even under war conditions, it was hard to kill such a boy. The Federals, it seems clear, went to remarkable lengths to provide him with an opportunity to escape. They wanted Coleman badly, of course, and yet there was something more . . .

Reluctantly Dodge ordered a court-martial in the courthouse. The prisoner was accused of spying, of going within Union lines for the purpose of "secretly gaining information" and taking it to the enemy. A second count called him a "carrier of mails, communications and information" from Union lines to persons in arms against the United States.

Sam Davis faced the older men. He was innocent of spying, he said; but he admitted carrying Southern information. He had a single defense. He had entered only as a military scout, with a Southern pass in his pocket, as they knew; his costume had been that of a Confederate, and he had worn no insignia of the Union. Therefore he should be regarded simply as a prisoner of war.

The grave soldier judges listened with care, taking down the opinions for and against Sam. In their eyes, however, the verdict was obvious—guilty. The sentence was hanging, on November 27, 1863, the day after Thanksgiving.

Through Thanksgiving day the Union officers continued their efforts to persuade Sam to speak. A middle-aged townswoman who knew the Davis family asked permission to see him. When she failed to change his mind, she went to Dodge himself to beg the general somehow to spare the boy. Other people added their appeals. The general said he could not: "A soldier caught in the uniform, or part of the uniform, of his enemy, within his enemy's lines, establishes the fact that he is a spy."

Still Sam's leader, Captain Shaw, watched developments anxiously. Might Sam break at the last minute? Among the prisoners many were certain that he would.

In spite of the holiday festivity, a number of the staff members felt the weight of the impending execution. On Thanksgiving night the chaplain visited Sam, and they sat together for a long time, talking softly. Then they prayed. Sam asked Chaplain Young if they could sing a hymn. The chaplain nodded, and the condemned youth chose "Land of Promise," a favorite of his mother's.

The music drifted through the jail, and the other prisoners listened. Among them was Shaw, now sad and silent, his eyes on the boy in the dim corner of the building. That night Sam thought again of the family he had left a few days before, and wrote:

> Dear Mother: Oh, how painful it is to write you! I have got to die tomorrow—to be hanged by the Federals. Mother, do not grieve for me. I must bid you good-by for evermore. Mother, I do not fear to die. Give my love to all.
>
> Your dear son.

The day after Thanksgiving was chill and dark, and it did not improve as the hours passed. By 10 A.M. Provost Marshal Armstrong had arrived with a wagon, on it a plain new pine coffin. Sam's eyes turned to the windows at which his fellow Confederates, Shaw and the others, were watching. With his manacled hands, he saluted them, and Henry Shaw's head dropped.

The boy sat on the top of his coffin. The procession moved through the main street of the town, to the muffled roll of drums, and stopped at the ridge just outside town limits. There the XVI Army Corps lined up to form a hollow square before a tree with a scaffold.

After the wagon jolted to a halt, Sam Davis got out and

sat on the ground. He faced the provost marshal: "How long do I have, Captain?"

"About fifteen minutes."

The youth's face was impassive. "What's the news from the front?"

"Bragg lost at Lookout Mountain, Sam."

This time the eyes lowered. "I'm sorry. The boys will have to fight the rest of the battles without me."

The marshal started to collect Sam's personal belongings to be forwarded to his mother and sisters, when suddenly the group about the gallows heard a commotion. A man on a horse rode up, a paper in his hand. "Stop the execution, stop!" He was Dodge's chief scout, and he had timed his arrival for the maximum effect on the prisoner.

Jumping off the horse, the scout went to the boy and held out a pardon. Sam could have it, with a safe conduct to the Confederate lines, if he would give the name of his informant. The listeners could not hear all the conversation, but they clearly heard what Sam Davis said when he ended the interview. For the first time he spoke in anger: "Do you think I'd betray a friend?"

He had a last few minutes, and he spent them writing another note to his mother, while the chaplain sang the hymn he had chosen:

> "On Jordan's stormy banks I stand
> And cast a wistful eye
> To Canaan's fair and happy land. . . ."

Then Sam turned. "I'm ready." As his body swung, he started on his way to the "land of promise" that he had chosen.

The **Davis family** held no resentment toward their boy's

friend, Henry Shaw. After the war he lived for a time with Sam's half brother and went into business with him; ironically, he died with that other Davis in a steamboat explosion. To those who said that Shaw might have come forward to take the responsibility in the case, the Davises pointed out several facts. Shaw had many assistants; had he spoken they, too, might have been tracked down, and more men would have suffered. Sam had made his choice, dying so that his friends might live.

In the town of his execution an avenue has been named for Sam Davis, a marker erected to him; a monument has been placed on the grounds of the state capitol in Nashville. The state has purchased the Davis home as a memorial, which is visited annually by thousands. Among those who contributed to the Nashville monument was Union General Dodge.

He had done all he could to save Sam Davis, the general said, "but it was one of the fates of war, which is cruelty itself, and there is no refining it." The statue in Nashville bears the words attributed to the boy: "If I had a thousand lives, I would lose them all here before I would betray my friend or the confidence of my informer." General Dodge, the man who had him hanged, said simply, "He was too brave to die."

Corporal Hardy

BY RICHARD ELY DANIELSON

In those days, during the haying season, it was my duty to keep the men in the fields supplied with sufficient cooling drink to enable them to support the heat and burden of the day. According to our established practice, this cooling drink consisted of cold water from the spring, flavored, for some obscure New England reason, with molasses, and it had to be freshly renewed every hour. We had plenty of ice in the icehouse, but there was a stubborn tradition that ice water was bad for men working in hayfields under the hot sun.

So every hour I carried down a brown jug containing the innocent mixture of molasses 'n' water to the hands, each one of whom would pause in his work, throw the jug over his upper arm, drink deeply thereof, wipe the sweat off his forehead, say "Thanks, Bub," and go on making hay. I was only ten years old, but it was no hardship to carry the jug, and it was fun to see their Adam's apples working as they drank.

This was routine practice on our Connecticut farm. Mostly the farm hands—hired men, we called them—came back to the house at noon and ate in the kitchen, after washing up at the pump outside. But in haymaking season each man sought a patch of shade, and his meal was carried to him there, to be eaten in the fields. I suppose the men's overheated bodies cooled off in the wisps of breeze drifting across the scorching mowings more effectively and comfortably than would have been possible in a hot summer kitchen. I am sure that my father did everything he could to make their lot as comfortable and healthy as possible. He worked with them, under the same conditions, setting them an example of careful, efficient labor. He differed from his men only in the fact that he was always cleanly shaved, that he gave orders and directions, and that he wore a silk shirt even in the hayfields. Nobody objected in the least to this token, for he was the owner, and he had been to college, and everyone admitted that he was fair and square.

On such occasions, when the men were given their dinners out of doors, I always carried his victuals to Mr. Hardy, because I liked to sit with him while he ate and listen to his stories. I think he enjoyed talking, in his racy Connecticut vernacular, to such a fascinated audience of one. He was a Civil War veteran, like my father, who, however, had been too young to enlist until the last year of the war and had seen almost no active service. But

Mr. Hardy was a soldier. Congress had given him a medal
—of honor—and all men regarded him with respect.

As I look back and remember his stories, I think he
must have been the most modest man I have ever known.
Certainly he never thought of himself as a hero. He would
accept no pension. "I'm able-bodied. I can work, can't
I?" But, alas, he was not really able-bodied. He had been
grievously wounded several times, and in 1895, when I
fetched and carried for him and sat at his feet, it was pitiful to see his valiant efforts to fork hay on the wagon or
do the other farming tasks which required muscular
strength. He was thin and bent, but his face was brown
and clean and his blue eyes bright and indomitable.

My father employed Mr. Hardy whenever there was
work to give him, and treated him—I did not, at that time,
know why—differently from the other hired men. He was
poor, he lived alone, he was unsuccessful, and in New
England then we rated people by their comparative success. But he worked stoutly and asked no favors of anyone.
It was generally conceded that Mr. Hardy, if a failure,
was nevertheless a good man.

I remember the last day I served him. I brought him his
dinner in a basket—cold meat 'n' potatoes, 'n' bread 'n' but-
ter, 'n' cold coffee, 'n' pie. He was seated in the shade of an
oak tree, leaning against a stack of hay. I put the food
down beside him and sat down, hugging my knees and
rocking back and forth. It was pleasant there, with the
smell of the hay and the drone of the bees, and the good,
warm feeling of the earth.

Mr. Hardy lay back against the haymow. "Thanks,
Jackie," he said. "I don't seem to be hungry today. It's hot
and this tree don't give much shade. Why, dammit, it's like
that mean little oak tree down to Chancellorsville."

I said, "Oh, Mr. Hardy, you've told me about Antietam and the Wilderness, but you've never told me about Chancellorsville. What was it like?"

He said slowly, "I ain't never told nobody about Chancellorsville, and I don't aim to tell nobody—grown-up, that is. But I'd kind of like to tell somebody that don't know nothing—like you—about it, for the first and last time. You'll forget it, and it would kind of ease my mind."

Mr. Hardy hoisted himself a little higher on the haymow and made a pretense of eating some bread and meat.

"Chancellorsville," he said, "was a bad battle, an awful bad battle. We didn't fight good and they was too many of them and I lost my captain."

"Who was he?" I asked.

"Why," he said, incredulously, "you oughta know that! He was Captain William Armstrong, commandin' Company B, 39th Connecticut. 'N' his twin brother, Ezra, was lootenant. He was younger by an hour or so, and they was identical twins. They never was two men as much alike—in looks, that is, for they was quite unlike inside. The lootenant was always stompin' around an' shoutin' an' wavin' his arms, an' the captain, he was always quiet an' soft-spoken an' brave an' gentle. He was a good man—he was an awful good man. I guess he was the best man I ever knowed."

He paused and took a sip of his cold coffee. Then he said, "Why, when we come to leave town to go in the cars to Hartford and then to Washington, their father—he was old Judge Armstrong, who lived in that big place up on Armstrong Hill—the Judge come up to me and says, 'Nathan, you look after my boys,' he said. 'They're younger than you be. You kind of keep an eye on them, for my sake,' he says. 'They is good boys,' he says. 'I will, Judge,'

I says. 'I'll do my best.' An' he says to me, 'I know you will, Nathan Hardy.' "

"But tell me, Mr. Hardy," I broke in, for I was not interested in the Armstrong twins, "what happened at Chancellorsville?"

"It was a bad battle, as I said. Them Rebs came charging out of the woods, hollerin' and yellin' and helligolar-rupin', and they was too many of them. The lootenant, he kept stomping up and down, shouting, 'Never give ground, boys! Stay where you are! Take careful aim! Never retreat!' Those was his words. I will never forget them, because he meant them. But my captain—I was next to him—says, 'They're too many; we can't stop 'em. Tell the men to retreat slowly, firing as often as they can reload.' Just then it hit him right in the chest. *Thunk* was the noise it made; just like thet—*thunk!* I caught him as he fell, and the blood began to come out of his mouth. He tried to speak, but he was vomiting blood dreadful, so all he could do was to make faces, and his lips said, 'Tell Elizabeth. . . .' and then he died. I put him down and noticed we was under a mean little oak tree on the edge of our trenches.

"Then they was around us, hairy men with bayonets, stabbin' and shootin' and yellin', and we soldiers had kind of drifted together in groups and the lootenant was shouting, 'Don't retreat, men!' and he got hit right in the knee and fell down; and so I picked him up and put him across my shoulder and started for the rear. He kep' hittin' me in the face and swearing, 'You damn coward! You left my brother there and you're making me retreat!' I says to him, 'Ezra, be reasonable; I'm takin' you to an ambulance. You ain't fit to fight, and as soon as I can I'm goin' back to bury William. They ain't goin' to shovel him into no trench,' I said. So he stopped hitting at me.

"I was strong then, and I musta carried him a mile or a mile and a few rods when we come to some stretcher men near a house, and I said, 'You take this officer to the nearest surgeon. They got to saw his leg off.' And they said, 'We ain't carryin' no wounded. We're a burial detail.' I said, pulling my pistol out, 'You will be if you don't carry this man. I'm kind of tuckered, but I ain't too tuckered to shoot.' So two of them carried him, and I went along with my pistol till we come to a place where surgeons was carving men up and I handed over the lootenant. He come to as I did so, and said, 'You scoundrel, you made me retreat. I'll never forgive you!' I said, 'Ezra, they're going to saw your leg off and you'll never fight again, but I'll bury William if it's the last thing I do.' He says, 'Is that a promise?' And I says, 'That's a promise. But it ain't a promise to you—it's one I made to your pa.'

"So I stayed with him and helped hold him while they sawed his leg off. They havin' run out of chloroform, it took four of us to hold him. And when it was over he was unconscious, and they put him in a cart with some others and took him away. So I went back to the house where the burial men were loafing. It was pretty ruined, but I found a shingle that was almos' clean and I wrote on it, in the light of a fire, 'cause it was dark then:

CAPT. WILLIAM ARMSTRONG
Commanding Co. B., 39th Connecticut
He was an awful good man

"Then I borrowed a spade from this burial party. We had an argument about it, but I persuaded them with my pistol and I started off toward the Rebel lines. I hadn't gone very far when I come to a place which was thick with men moanin' and screamin' and lots that wasn't sayin' nothing at all. I didn't want to walk on them an' I couldn't help them, having nothing on me but a shingle and a spade and a pistol, an' I decided I couldn't find the captain in the dark anyhow, so I set down and tried to sleep, for I was tuckered. I threw away my pistol. I set there the rest of the night waitin' for the dawn. It was a long time comin'.

"When it come gray, I started out with my shingle and my spade and I went along till I was challenged by the Rebel pickets and sentries. I answered, 'Union burial detail. I'm comin' for to bury my captain.' They begun shootin' at me and I don't know as I blame them. I was comin' out of the mist and they couldn't see that I was alone an' wasn't armed. So they shot real hard, and one bullet struck me in the left thigh and I fell down. Fortunately I had a belt, and I sat up and took it off and strapped it real tight over my wound, and my britches was tight at the waist so they didn't come down, and I got up and went on.

"They stopped shootin' and a man with a bayonet got up and said, 'Yank, you're my pris'ner.' And I said, 'I know I be, but I ain't your pris'ner till I bury my captain.' And I held up my shingle and spade. He said, 'Where's he lie?' And I said, 'About a quarter mile from here and maybe a few rods, under a mean little oak tree; and,' I says, 'you take me there and I'll bury him and then I'm your pris'ner. They ain't goin' to stuff my captain into no ditch,' I says. He says, 'You may be crazy, Yank, or you may be a spy. You come with me an' I'll turn you over to the captain.'

" 'Your captain alive?' I asks.

" 'I reckon so,' he says.

" 'Mine's dead,' I says, 'and I aim for to bury him.'

"So he tuk me away with his bayonet in my back and the blood was squilchin' in my boot, but I got along to where his captain was and the captain asked questions, and the Rebel soldier, he tol' all he knew, an' the captain says, 'Where's he lie?' An' I says, 'By a mean little oak, where our lines was yesterday mornin'.'

"An' the captain says, 'That ain't far away. I'll send a detail to bury him.' I says, 'Ain't nobody goin' to bury the captain but me,' I says. 'After that, I'll be your pris'ner.'

"They was a young man dressed up all pretty with gold braid on his uniform, and he laughed kind of loud and he says, 'Saves us the trouble of buryin' him!' an' the captain turns on him, real stern, and says, 'Lootenant, this is a brave soldier,' he says, 'who come back under fire and was wounded to bury his company commander and give himself up as pris'ner. I will not have him insulted or laughed at,' he says. Then he turns to me an' says, 'What is your name an' rank?'

" 'Corporal Nathan Hardy, Co. B, 39th Connecticut,' I says.

"An' he says, 'Corporal, you and I an' these men,' turnin' around to the five or six Rebs who was listenin', 'will go together to find your captain.'

"So we went and I found him, underneath that mean little oak tree, and he looked dreadful. His eyes was open and they was an awful lot of blood on his shirt where his coat was open, and he was lyin' all sprangled out an' undignified. An' the first thing I done was to straighten him out. I spit on my sleeve and wiped the blood off his mouth the best I could. An' I closed his eyes an' buttoned his coat an' crossed his arms. They was kind of stiff, but I done it, an' I brushed him off and laid him out regular.

"Then I started diggin', and it would have been easy if it hadn't been for my leg and all the blood in my boot. Six foot four or thereabouts it was, and three foot deep—not as deep as I wanted, but I couldn't dig no deeper. I was so tuckered. But it was an honest grave, for I was real handy with a spade in them days. Then I stood up and said, 'Will two o' you Rebs hand the captain to me?' Which they done, and I laid him in the grave. An' as I stood lookin' down at him lyin' there, I says to myself, 'Ain't nobody goin' to shovel no dirt on the captain's face—nobody, nobody, nobody at all, not even me!' So I took my coat off and laid it over him, coverin' up his face best I could. I didn't want to go to no Rebel prison in my shirt, but I wouldn't have no one shovel dirt on the captain.

"Then the two Rebs pulled me out of the grave, real gentle and considerate. An' then I noticed they was a Rebel general there sittin' on a blood horse. How long he bin there I don't know. He looked at me and see I was wounded and peaked, and he says, stern an' hard, 'Captain, what's the meanin' of this? This man's wounded and weak,' he says. 'Do you force wounded men to bury the dead?'

"The captain went over to him and began talkin' to him low and earnest, seemed like, all the time I was fillin' in the grave. An' when I patted the mound even, so it looked good, and had stuck the shingle in the new earth at the head of the grave, I come over to where the general was, limpin' and leanin' on my spade, an' I saluted—couldn't help it; I kind of forgot he was a Rebel—an' I says, 'General, I'm your pris'ner. I buried my captain. I ain't a great hand at askin' favors, an' your captain and these Rebs has been real good to me. But I wanta ask one more. I was

raised Episcopal, which was unusual in our town, and so
was the captain. I'd kind of like to say a prayer before I
surrender . . .' "

Here Mr. Hardy seemed to doze for a little. "Where was
I?" he asked, rousing after a few minutes.

"You had just gone up to the general and asked if you
could say a prayer before you surrendered."

"Yes, yes, so it was. The general said, 'Corporal Hardy,
I am an Episcopalian too, and you shall say your prayer.'

"So he dismounted and took off his hat, and he and I
kneeled down by the grave, and it was awful hard for me
to kneel. And when we was there kneelin' I looked up for
a minute and all them Rebs was standin' with their caps
off and their heads bowed, nice and decent, just like
Northern people. An' then I had a dreadful time, for to save
my life I couldn't remember a prayer, not a line, not a
word. I had heard the burial service often enough and
too often, what with Pa and Ma an' all kinds of relatives,
but my brains was all watery an' thin, nothin' at all. I
don't know how long 'twas till somethin' come driftin' into
my mind. It wa'n't from the burial service; 'twas somethin'
we used to chant in Evenin' Prayer. So I says it, loud as I
could, for I was gettin' awful feeble.

" 'Lord,' I says, 'now lettest Thou Thy servant depart in
peace, according to Thy Word. . . .' An' I couldn't remember to say any more. The general, he helped me to my
feet, spade an' all, an' I looked him in the face and, by
creepers, they was tears in his beard. Soon as I could speak
I says, 'General, you've been real good to me and I thank
you. An' now I'm your pris'ner, wherever you want to send
me.'

"An' he says, 'Corporal Hardy, you will never be a pris'ner of our people as long as I live and command this corps.'

"An' I broke in, awful scared he had misunderstood, and I says, 'General, you don't think I was prayin' for *me* to go in peace! I'm your pris'ner; I'm not askin' for no favors. I was thinkin' of the captain—and me too, perhaps, but not that way. I can go anywhere now. I—'

"He cut me short. 'Corporal Hardy,' he says, 'I know to Whom you was prayin' and why, an' I haven't misunderstood you at all. Captain,' he says, 'I want a detail of six men an' a stretcher and a flag of truce to take this brave soldier an'—an' Christian gentleman back to the Union lines; an' I want this message, which I have dictated and signed, delivered to the commanding officer to be forwarded through channels to the Secretary of War or the President. Those people can hardly decline this courtesy, under the circumstances . . . Wait, Carter, I wish to add a few lines.' So he put the paper against his saddle and he wrote for some time.

"Then, kind of in a dream, I heard the Rebel captain say, 'Sir, if the General permits, I would like to lead this detail to the Union lines and ask to be blindfolded and deliver your message to the Division Commander.'

"An' the General says, 'Captain, I am very glad you made that request, and I commend your behavior. It is only fittin' that the officer escortin' Corporal Hardy with my message should be of field rank, and I shall put in my order for your promotion. You are a pretty good soldier, yourself,' he says—only he didn't say it that way.

"All this time I was kind of waverin' around, but I heard most all they said; and because I was feeble from losing blood an' the battle an' buryin' the captain an' a kind of feverish feelin', things begun to spin around, and I started walkin' this way and that way with my spade, tryin' to stand up, knowin' I couldn't much longer. I heard someone yell 'Catch him!' An' the next thing I knowed I was in a bed of straw and they was probin' for the bullet in my leg. Then I don't remember nothin' till I woke up in a bed, a clean bed, with a nice-lookin' woman leanin' over me, wipin' my head with a cold, wet towel. I says, 'Where am I?'

"An' she says, 'You're in the hospital of the Sanitary Commission in Washington. An' oh, Corporal Hardy,' she says, 'I'm so glad you're conscious, for today the President is comin' to give you the Medal of Honor.' An' I says, 'Listen, sister, I gotta get out of here. I don't care for no President or no medal—I gotta bury the captain. He's lyin' down there under a mean little oak. Gimme my clothes,' I says. 'I want a spade and a shingle.' An' she says, 'Corporal, you buried your captain an' buried him fine. That's why the President is comin' to see you. Now you just drink this and go to sleep for a while, and I'll wake you when the President comes.'

"So I drank it and kind of slept, and when I woke up there was Old Abe, the ugliest man I ever see, leanin' over and pinnin' something to my nightshirt, an' he says, 'Corporal Hardy, even the enemy call you a brave soldier and a good man. Congress has voted you this medal. God bless you,' he says."

Mr. Hardy yawned and closed his eyes, and leaned against the haymow. He had told the tale he had to tell— once, to one person.

"But, Mr. Hardy," I said, "what happened to the lieutenant, and who was Elizabeth?" I wanted the story all tied up in ribbons.

"Who?" he said. "The lootenant? Oh, Ezra come back and married Elizabeth and they went to live in Massachusetts. Seems he went aroun' sayin' he couldn't live in no town where people pointed at him and thought he had run away leavin' his dead brother. Naturally no one done so or thought so. But, for all his stompin' and shoutin', he was sensitive, an' he bore me a grudge for takin' him away. I don't see as how I could a done different. I'd promised the old Judge I'd look after his boys an' I've allus aimed to keep my promises."

Just then my father came up to us. It was unlike Mr. Hardy to sit in the shade while other men had started to work again, and Father looked worried. "How are you feeling, Nathan?" he asked.

"Why, John, I'm plumb tuckered out, and that's a fact. I don't know as I can do much more work today. Seems like I never did fare good under these mean little oak trees," and he glanced sharply at me with an expression that was almost a wink. We shared a secret.

Father looked startled, as if he thought Mr. Hardy's wits were wandering.

"I tell you what, Nathan," he said, "you've had all the sun you need. I'll send the wagon and they'll take you up to the house, where you can be cool and rest for a while." And, for once in his life, Mr. Hardy made no protest over having favors done for him. Father took me aside. "Jackie," he said, "you run up to the house and tell your mother to make the bed in the spare room ready, and then you go to the village and tell Dr. Fordyce he's wanted. I don't like Nathan's looks."

Before I started running I glanced at Mr. Hardy, and I

saw what Father meant. He was pale and flushed in the wrong places, though I hadn't noticed it at all when he was telling me about Chancellorsville.

So Mr. Hardy was put to bed in the spare room, and given such care and aid as we knew how to give. For several days he lay quietly enough, and, as I look back on it after all these years, I think that the weight and burden of his long, valiant struggle must suddenly have proved too great. He couldn't go on forever. Mr. Hardy was tuckered out.

Then for some time he alternated between unconsciousness and a mild delirium. He kept mumbling phrases: "Take that quid out o' your mouth. 'Tain't soldierly!" . . . "Ain't nobody goin' to bury the captain but me." I knew what lots of his bewildered sayings meant, but there were many which were obscure. I sat with him every day for an hour or so when the rest of the household were busy, and I had instructions to call my elders if Mr. Hardy needed help or became conscious.

One day he opened his eyes and said, "Here I am and I'm real easy in my mind—but I can't just remember what I said." I went out and called my parents, who told me to stay outside. But I listened and I heard Mr. Hardy say, "Call the boy in. He knows what I want said and I can't remember. He's young and 'twon't hurt him and he'll forget." So Mother beckoned me to come in and I said, "What can I do, Mr. Hardy?"

"You can say what I said for the captain when I knelt down with the general."

So I knelt down, and, having the parrotlike memory of childhood, I said, "You knelt down and so did the general, and then you couldn't remember any of the words of the burial service, but you did remember something that was

sung in the evening, and you said, 'Lord, now lettest Thou Thy servant depart in peace, according to Thy Word . . .'"
And I began to cry.

"That's right," he said very faintly, "that's right; that's it. Yes, Captain. . . ."

My mother gathered me up and took me out and held me very close, rocking back and forth with me while I wept out how I loved Mr. Hardy and what a good man he was.

And that was why I was sent to my aunt and cousins at New London, where I could swim and fish and forget about battles and wounds and Mr. Hardy. But I didn't forget.

Lincoln Speaks at Gettysburg

BY CARL SANDBURG

A printed invitation came to Lincoln's hands, notifying him
that on Thursday, November 19, 1863, exercises would be
held for the dedication of a National Soldiers' Cemetery
at Gettysburg. In the helpless onrush of the war too many
of the fallen had lain as neglected cadavers rotting in the
open fields or thrust into so shallow a resting place that a
common farm plow caught in their bones. Now, by order
of Governor Curtin of Pennsylvania, seventeen acres had
been purchased on Cemetery Hill, where the Union center
stood its colors on the second and third of July, and plots of
soil had been allotted each State for its graves.

The sacred and delicate duties of orator of the day had
fallen on Edward Everett, perhaps foremost of all distin-

guished American classical orators. Serene, suave, handsomely venerable in his sixty-ninth year, a prominent specimen of Northern upper-class distinction, Everett was a natural choice of the Pennsylvania commissioners, who sought an orator for a solemn national occasion.

Lincoln, meanwhile, in reply to the printed circular invitation, sent word to the commissioners that he would be present at the ceremonies. This made it necessary for the commissioners to consider whether the President should be asked to deliver an address when present.

And so on November 2, David Wills of Gettysburg, as the special agent of Governor Curtin and also acting for the several States, by letter informed Lincoln that the several States having soldiers in the Army of the Potomac who were killed, or had since died at hospitals in the vicinity, had procured grounds for a cemetery and proper burial of their dead. "These grounds will be consecrated and set apart to this sacred purpose by appropriate ceremonies on Thursday, the 19th instant. I am authorized by the Governors of the various States to invite you to be present and participate in these ceremonies, which will doubtless be very imposing and solemnly impressive. It is the desire that after the oration, you, as Chief Executive of the nation, formally set apart these grounds to their sacred use by a few appropriate remarks."

Fifteen thousand—some said thirty thousand or fifty thousand—people were on Cemetery Hill for the exercises on November 19. On the platform sat governors, major generals, foreign ministers, members of Congress, officials, together with Colonel Ward Hill Lamon, Edward Everett and his daughter, and the President of the United States.

The United States House chaplain offered a prayer while the thousands stood with uncovered heads.

Benjamin B. French, officer in charge of buildings in Washington, introduced the Honorable Edward Everett, orator of the day, who rose, and bowed low to Lincoln, saying, "Mr. President." Lincoln responded, "Mr. Everett."

The orator of the day then stood in silence before a crowd that stretched to limits that would test his voice. Beyond and around were the wheat fields, the meadows, the peach orchards, long slopes of land, and, five and seven miles farther, the contemplative blue ridge of a low mountain range. His eyes could sweep them as he faced the audience. He had taken note of it in his prepared and rehearsed address. "Overlooking these broad fields now reposing from the labors of the waning year, the mighty Alleghenies dimly towering before us, the graves of our brethren beneath our feet, it is with hesitation that I raise my poor voice to break the eloquent silence of God and Nature. But the duty to which you have called me must be performed;—grant me, I pray you, your indulgence and your sympathy." He spoke for an hour and fifty-seven minutes, some said a trifle over two hours, repeating almost word for word an address that occupied nearly two news-paper pages, as he had written it and as it had gone in ad-vance sheets to many newspapers.

Everett came to his closing sentence without a faltering voice: "Down to the latest period of recorded time, in the glorious annals of our common country there will be no brighter page than that which relates the Battles of Gettysburg." It was the effort of his life and embodied the perfections of the school of oratory in which he had spent his career. His erect form and sturdy shoulders, his white hair and head flung back at dramatic points, his voice, his poise, and chiefly some quality of inside goodhearted-ness, held most of his audience to him, though the people in the front rows had taken their seats three hours before his oration closed.

Having read Everett's address, Lincoln knew when the moment drew near for him to speak. He took out his own manuscript from a coat pocket, put on his steel-bowed glasses, stirred in his chair, looked over the manuscript, and put it back in his pocket. Ward Hill Lamon rose and spoke the words, "The President of the United States," who rose, and holding in one hand the two sheets of paper at which he occasionally glanced, delivered the address in his high-pitched and clear-carrying voice.

Four score and seven years ago our fathers brought forth on this continent a new nation conceived in liberty and dedicated to the proposition that all men are created equal.

Now we are engaged in a great civil war testing whether that nation, or any nation so conceived and so dedicated, can long endure. We are met on a great battlefield of that war. We have come to dedicate a portion of that field as a final resting place for those who here gave their lives that that nation might live.

It is altogether fitting and proper that we should do this. But, in a larger sense, we cannot dedicate, we cannot consecrate, we cannot hallow this ground. The brave men, living and dead, who struggled here have consecrated it far above our poor power to add or detract. The world will little note nor long remember what we say here, but it can never forget what they did here.

It is for us the living rather to be dedicated here to the unfinished work which they who fought here have thus far so nobly advanced. It is rather for us to be

here dedicated to the great task remaining before us—
that from these honored dead we take increased devotion to that cause for which they gave the last full
measure of devotion—that we here highly resolve that
these dead shall not have died in vain, that this nation under God shall have a new birth of freedom,
and that government of the people, by the people, for
the people, shall not perish from the earth.

The applause, according to most of the responsible wit-
nesses, was formal and perfunctory, a tribute to the occasion, to the high office, to the array of important men of
the nation on the platform, by persons who had sat as an
audience for three hours. Ten sentences had been spoken
in five minutes, and some were surprised that it should end
before the orator had really begun to get his outdoor voice.

The ride to Washington took until midnight. Lincoln was
weary, talked little.

He had stood that day, the world's foremost spokesman
of popular government, saying that democracy was yet
worth fighting for. He had spoken as one in mist who might
head on deeper yet into mist. He incarnated the assurances
and pretenses of popular government, implied that it
could and might perish from the earth. What he meant by
"a new birth of freedom" for the nation could have a thousand interpretations. The taller riddles of democracy stood
up out of the address. It had the dream touch of vast and
furious events epitomized for any foreteller to read what
was to come. He did not assume that the drafted soldiers,
substitutes, and bounty-paid privates had died willingly
under Lee's shot and shell, in deliberate consecration of
themselves to the Union cause. His cadences sang the
ancient song that where there is freedom men have fought

and sacrificed for it, and that freedom is worth men's dying for. For the first time since he became President he had on a dramatic occasion declaimed, howsoever it might be read, Jefferson's proposition which had been a slogan of the Revolutionary War—"All men are created equal"—leaving no other inference than that he regarded the Negro slave as a man. His outwardly smooth sentences were inside of them gnarled and tough with the enigmas of the American Experiment.

Back at Gettysburg the blue haze of the Cumberland Mountains had dimmed till it was a blur in a nocturne. The moon was up and fell with a bland golden benevolence on the new-made graves of soldiers, on the sepulchers of old settlers, on the horse carcasses of which the onrush of war had not yet permitted removal.

In many a country cottage over the land, a tall old clock in a quiet corner told time in a tick-tock deliberation. Whether the orchard branches hung with pink-spray blossoms or icicles of sleet, whether the outside news was seedtime or harvest, rain or drouth, births or deaths, the swing of the pendulum was right and left and right and left with a tick-tock deliberation.

The face and dial of the clock had known the eyes of a boy who listened to its tick-tock and learned to read its minute and hour hands. And the boy had seen years measured off by the swinging pendulum, and grown to man size, had gone away. And the people in the cottage knew that the clock would stand there and the boy never again come into the room and look at the clock with the query, "What is the time?"

In a row of graves of the Unidentified the boy would sleep long in the dedicated final resting place at Gettysburg. Why he had gone away and why he would never come back had roots in some mystery of flags and drums, of national fate in which individuals sink as in a deep sea, of men swallowed and vanished in a man-made storm of smoke and steel.

The mystery deepened and moved with ancient music and inviolable consolation because a solemn Man of Authority had stood at the graves of the Unidentified and spoken the words: "We cannot consecrate, we cannot hallow, this ground. The brave men, living and dead, who struggled here have consecrated it far above our poor power to add or detract . . . From these honored dead we take increased devotion to that cause for which they gave the last full measure of devotion."

To the backward and forward pendulum swing of a tall old clock in a quiet corner they might read those cadenced words, while outside the windows the first flurry of snow blew across the orchard and down over the meadow, the beginnings of winter in a gun-metal gloaming to be later arched with a star-flung sky.